PENGUIN CRIME FICTION

SINGAPORE TRANSFER

Wayne Warga is the author of two previous Jeffrey
Dean mysteries, *Hardcover* and *Fatal Impressions*. A
former *Life* magazine correspondent in Cuba and
Central America, he has also written for the *Los
Angeles Times*, *Entertainment Tonight*, and *USA
Today: On TV*. He collects modern first editions and
contemporary art, and lives in Studio City, California.

Singapore Transfer

WAYNE WARGA

A Jeffrey Dean mystery

PENGUIN BOOKS

PENGUIN BOOKS
Published by the Penguin Group
Viking Penguin, a division of Penguin Books USA Inc.,
375 Hudson Street, New York, New York 10014, U.S.A.
Penguin Books Ltd, 27 Wrights Lane,
London W8 5TZ, England
Penguin Books Australia Ltd, Ringwood,
Victoria, Australia
Penguin Books Canada Ltd, 10 Alcorn Avenue, Suite 300,
Toronto, Ontario, Canada M4V 3B2
Penguin Books (N.Z.) Ltd, 182–190 Wairau Road,
Auckland 10, New Zealand

Penguin Books Ltd, Registered Offices:
Harmondsworth, Middlesex, England

First published in the United States of America by
Viking Penguin, a division of
Penguin Books USA Inc., 1991
Published in Penguin Books 1992

1 3 5 7 9 10 8 6 4 2

Copyright © Jake Enterprises, Ltd., 1991
All rights reserved

THE LIBRARY OF CONGRESS HAS CATALOGUED THE HARDCOVER AS FOLLOWS:
Warga, Wayne.
Singapore transfer / Wayne Warga.
p.   cm.
ISBN 0-670-83569-2 (hc.)
ISBN 0 14 01.4383 1 (pbk.)
I. Title.
PS3573.A755S56   1991
813'.54—dc20   90–50753

Printed in the United States of America
Set in Times Roman

For
Carol
with love

Singapore Transfer

1

This is how he remembered it. Not as a journalist might carefully reconstruct events, not as a methodical man might have noted most of it in his pocket diary. Jeffrey Dean was both these things, but as he continually had to remind himself, he was also a man in distress.

He was in Washington for several reasons. It was, he told himself, the perfect opportunity. He had come in response to a series of telephone calls from a man with whom he had worked many times before and whom he respected greatly. Jeffrey was one of a small team of men and women assembled by his friend to rescue a disastrous experiment in television news. The challenge had appealed to him, all the more so because it was only a short-term project—November through February—which would include the two crucial TV ratings months.

Also, he had grown bored and restless with his rare-book business. The call had come at a crucial moment: he and Rachel were becoming increasingly enclosed in their separate worlds. They had had an argument one night, one of those rare occasions of anger and acrimony when only silence well into the next day could even begin to undo the damage. She had used the expression first, and they both had hated it: He was, she said with a mixture of fear and offense, having a "midlife crisis."

To Jeffrey, it seemed worse: the angst was killing him. He was also missing the action of journalism and becoming bored with his book business. He wanted to get back into journalism, briefly and on his own terms.

His wish had come true almost immediately, and within three weeks he had found himself smiling grimly as one of the show's anchors was throwing yet another temper tantrum, minutes before the show itself, still not complete, was scheduled to go up on the satellite. As a commentary on the chaos, the anchor's neurotic dog had just shit on the newsroom floor. Be careful what you wish, he thought to himself, because you just might get it.

"You're making me look like an asshole in front of six million people," the anchorwoman screamed.

"Two million if you're lucky," someone at the news desk muttered.

Jeffrey finessed it, maneuvered the anchor into trying both versions of the contested script, "asshole and unasshole." Angry, she was shrill and unreasonable. On camera she was, as someone put it, forceful. Braying like a mule was more like it. On the floor scooping dogshit into copy paper she was, at least, slightly vulnerable. The trouble was, she had some intelligence, a genuine concern for her stories, and absolutely no sense of how awful she could be in person and on the air. Part of Jeffrey's job—*challenge* would be more like it—was to change that. Less than a month into it, he was already beginning to feel like Sisyphus.

The pay was terrific, and he was fascinated by Washington. He also had the backing of his friend, Craig Fellows, with whom he had worked before and whom Jeffrey considered responsible for the very best years of his career. And so, at a midcareer point in both of his chosen professions, Jeffrey found himself well paid, living at the Ritz Carlton Hotel, missing Rachel, missing his son Michael, yet somehow enjoying his solitude.

There was about him a slight air of formality, something reserved. He had grown up as a part of the "do your own thing" generation, and his own thing had turned out to be far from undisciplined and carefree. Now, in the waning months of his forty-first year, there were highlights of gray in his dark blond hair, and he had noticed to his dismay that there were gray hairs now on his chest and stomach. He was just under six feet tall, fit, with an attractive look and very watchful eyes. He had spent so many years observing and reporting that he sometimes thought he was observing his own life from a similarly detached point of view. He had married once, unsuccessfully, and was the father of a teenage son he adored. Then came Rachel.

Weekends in Washington, Jeffrey the journalist would become Jeffrey the rare-book dealer. From his hotel, which was just off Dupont Circle, he walked down P Street, across the bridge over Rock Creek Parkway, to prowl the bookstores in Georgetown. Other times he played tourist, taking the Metro to the Mall, visiting the Smithsonian, standing under the towering dome of the Library of Congress, or walking through the Capitol building.

Washington was fascinating, its cold winter air invigorating for a Californian. Jeffrey was seldom bored. This was the capital of the most powerful nation on earth, yet it was also a small Southern city. A deeply troubled city, for within a few short blocks of its perfectly impersonal government buildings were slums filled with poor blacks and streetcorners crowded with drug dealers. Washington, D.C., was a symbol of the free world, the best and the worst of it.

He hurried down P Street, carefully avoiding the ice patches on the sidewalk, and stepped into the warmth of Galileo, a slightly pretentious but nevertheless good Italian restaurant. He performed the unfamiliar winter ritual of removing his gloves, coat, and scarf, and handed them to the hostess. Then he sat down, opened the London *Times* he had ordered from the show's research library, and ordered wine, salad, and a large plate of linguine pesto. He permitted himself to feel very much a citizen of the world.

He was reading, with some amusement, an account of an

invasion of bees in England's largest nudist colony—when it occurred to him that one of the things he wanted to do before he left Washington was to go to an embassy party. Any embassy party, though he'd prefer one given by a Communist nation. The USSR would do.

But by the time he received an invitation it was nearly the end of February. He was relieved that he would soon be leaving Washington, and was looking forward to returning to Rachel and his business. Rachel had come to Washington for a long Thanksgiving holiday and had brought Michael along. At fifteen, Michael was an avid tourist; the three of them had walked the major sights of Washington, beginning with the Lincoln Memorial and the Vietnam Memorial wall on up the Mall to the Capitol and the National Arboretum. They hadn't missed one building along the way. Rachel had patiently regretted Jeffrey's need to be away for a while and had told him how much she loved him one night after they had made love.

"You belong with me," she had whispered to him, her breath sweet like the scent of her body.

"I know, I know. I sometimes just don't feel like I belong anywhere."

"But you do. I need you. Michael needs you. You belong to us."

She was right, and it was because he belonged and he knew it that he could indulge his wanderlust from time to time.

"It's the seven-year itch," she said. He could feel her lips moving on his chest.

"The what?"

"The seven-year itch."

"The Marilyn Monroe movie?"

"Yes. We've been together seven years now."

"Yeah, but in the movie Tom Euell was married."

Silence.

"We're not," he added for emphasis.

"We're the same as married."

"I suppose."

"No, really. We've been together seven years. Isn't that what makes a common-law marriage?"

"That's too common for me."

It was an old argument, if it could be called that. Rachel, at thirty-eight, was still adamant about her independence, even though she had surrendered part of it to him long ago. And he had happily relinquished his to her. That was how it had worked for them.

Neither felt passionate about getting married, but from time to time Jeffrey got the urge again. He was, at heart, a romantic. She was far more practical.

"It's working just fine, if you'd get over your wanderlust and come home."

"It'll be over at the end of February sweeps," he said to her, shifting his body slightly so that his face rested on her breasts.

"You want your cake and you want to eat it too."

"I already did that tonight."

"I wasn't talking about sex. I was talking about life."

"Uhmm." He was falling asleep.

The show itself was planned, primarily executed, assembled, and sent by satellite from the eighteenth floor of a high rise that overlooked all of Washington, D.C. Jeffrey and the two other writers sat along with the show's line producer at the big horseshoe desk surveying the newsroom kingdom where, one of the other writers observed one day, hardly anyone was ever seen reading a newspaper. To his rear was a panoramic view of northwest Washington, the National Cathedral, and the new Russian embassy complex atop Mount Alto. Jeffrey could even see the sea of shortwave aerials atop the embassy which, as yet, was unoccupied. The Russians were being punished for bugging every bit of brick and mortar in the new American embassy in Moscow.

There were also plenty of bugs in the *Today-Tomorrow!* building, but of a different sort. The high rise was experiencing a trend—largely unpublicized—involving pregnant women who worked at computer terminals suffering a sharply higher incidence of miscarriages than other women. The fear had also spread to the television show as well, though it was cynically assumed the women on the staff were too ambitious and had too little recreational time for getting pregnant. If that weren't trouble enough, the Health Department had come in and shut down all of the building's drinking fountains because of a high lead content which could lead to liver damage.

The trouble in the computers and in the plumbing also extended out over the airwaves. The anchors, who had been accustomed to saying whatever they wanted on the air, revolted immediately and irrationally against the attempt to salvage the show's disastrous debut. First, they refused the new scripts they were given. Then they agreed to read them, but changed them the moment they opened their mouths for the satellite feed. Finally, a sort of truce settled in, one that was constantly interrupted, but a truce nevertheless.

"You put a camera in front of these people and sooner or later you create a monster," Fellows had commented one night at dinner. He seemed to thrive on the chaos.

"Fire them," Jeffrey responded.

"I can't. They've got contracts."

"Look for windows. They've all got them somewhere."

"Oh, I know where they are."

"Defenestration for anchors is too good a way to die."

Fellows had smiled. "I hear Sam Donaldson is no easy person to work with."

"Maybe not. But at least he's good at what he does and he has years of network experience to back him up. These people haven't got much."

"Except their enormous salaries," Fellows added.

The show's owners had offered Jeffrey a permanent job—as permanent as it ever gets in that business—and a contract. He had politely declined.

It was time to go home to Rachel, the rare-book business, Rachel's gallery, the few remaining years with Michael before he was off to college and his own life. Jeffrey was to arrive back in Los Angeles the day before his forty-second birthday. And that, he believed, would be that. His great "midlife crisis" was ending; damn the pop psychologists who had invented the term and were harvesting a fortune in how-to books from it.

Before he was finished with his work on the show, he left the newsroom and took a cab to Britches, the yuppie citadel of Georgetown. There he looked in dismay at the sudden invasion of summer clothing in the worst month of winter. It always struck him as odd in California, but that was nothing compared to what a pair of loud Hawaiian-print shorts looked like on a dress dummy when the outside temperature was eighteen degrees and the Potomac was nearly frozen.

He settled on what he'd come for: a couple of cashmere sweaters sharply reduced to make way for the new season, and a new necktie. He intended to wear it to his first diplomatic social event at the Singapore embassy's chancery on R Street Northwest, just off Dupont Circle, and it was, as he had learned Singaporean celebrations tended to be, in honor of some new economic development—in this case, the arrival of Singapore Airlines at Dulles Airport.

He thought of it as a nice conclusion to his time in Washington. He was wrong. It was just the beginning.

2

"Would you like some help?"

"I was looking for something blue," she said, giving the fat Japanese shopkeeper what she hoped was a disarming and somewhat helpless look.

"Do you know birds?"

"No."

"How much would you like to spend?"

Leilani knew the reason for that question, knew very well why it was being asked. The superior airs of some Japanese, particularly those of relatively little education or position, seldom bothered her. She knew how to twist prejudice to her advantage, how to use the attitude of others toward Hawaiians as a kind of camouflage beneath which she moved and thought as she wished.

"How much is it possible to spend on a bird?"

"That parrot over there"—he gestured toward a vividly colored bird tied to a perch near the front of the store—"costs three hundred dollars."

Leilani shrugged and resumed browsing. She looked into each cage, hoping to spot the one odd bird that would be the clue she needed—something rare among the ordinary, and purposely mislabeled. When she came to a big cage of blue, yellow, and chartreuse parakeets, she scanned the birds carefully.

She saw it in a corner: a small, vividly blue bird with white jowls, a Tahitian lorry. Its value was considerable, all the more so because it was one of the two hundred lorries extant, a species hovering on the edge of extinction.

She smothered her elation and moved to the next cage, looked into it for a few seconds, then crossed to the other side of Toshiro's Pet Shoppe. As she passed the closed door to the back room, she could hear the muted calls of other birds.

"Are these all that you have?"

He looked just a bit insulted. She hoped so, because she wanted him to take the bait.

"This is it," he said with finality. He didn't even bite, she thought, and he is lying. That much she knew for sure. She stepped up to the expensive parrot, noticed the floor around it was littered with seed shells and shit. She smiled brightly at the shopkeeper.

"Are you Mr. Toshiro?"

"That's me."

"Does this parrot talk, Mr. Toshiro?"

"No, but he can be taught."

"Too bad he isn't blue," she said airily, starting for the door. "Well, thank you anyway."

Toshiro glared at her, said nothing, didn't even bother to nod. She had gotten to him and she knew it. She was certain the man didn't suspect her at all.

She grinned as she started out of the shopping center, and though she was shy about such things—sufficiently so to feel the blood start toward her cheeks at the thought—the image that sprang to mind nevertheless amused her. It was this: Toshiro, fat and arrogant, and the parrot, side by side, eating and shitting together. It was probably all either of them ever did. Except, that is, for Toshiro's sideline smuggling rare birds into Hawaii, a sideline that was about to be interrupted, to say the least.

She spotted a pay phone outside the supermarket. Toshiro—if he even deigned to look—couldn't see her make the call.

Mark O'Brien, chief of the Honolulu U.S. Treasury office, was on the line instantly, as she knew he would be.

"He's got one Tahitian lorry and there are birds he isn't showing," she said to him. "Let's shut him down."

"Think there'll be trouble?"

"I doubt it."

"Okay, I'll send help. Where will you be?"

"Pearl City Tavern."

"Okay. Good work."

"Thanks." She tried to sound appreciative, but wasn't sure she really did. She knew it was good work, knew that finding the bird was a coup of sorts. Fake humility was not her style, and she was too ambitious not to know the implications of her good work. She was very good at hiding her anger, and her ambition.

Leilani Martin succeeded not by emulating the *haole,* the white people—as the Orientals in Hawaii had done—but by emphasizing the fact that she was Hawaiian. Among her ancestors were an Irish sea captain, a Chinese cook, a Spanish sailor, all of whom married or had children by Hawaiian women. She was, in the vernacular of the islands, a calico, which meant she was also Hawaiian, one whose blood, though mixed, was predominantly Hawaiian. By her own rough calculation she was five-eighths native, and like many of her race, she was becoming increasingly conscious of her heritage.

She was also uncomfortably aware that she was a minority in her own land—only seventeen percent of the islanders could call themselves Hawaiian—and that she was a symbol: she was intelligent, educated, employed, and very well paid by the standards of her people. Hawaiians tended to earn their living shaking their hips to entertain tourists, or changing their beds in hotels. That was the common perception, and it was not far from the unpleasant truth.

Leilani was different. She was ambitious, and like many ambitious people, she could be ruthless. She seldom suffered from moral qualms, only from a fear of not succeeding on her terms. As a United States Customs Special Agent with six years' experience she earned $35,000 a year, more than both of her parents combined. Her education in fine arts qualified her to be a member of the U.S. Customs National Patrimony Unit. She was the bureau's expert on art, and the Patrimony Unit was charged with protection of what belonged to America. It was, in fact, a nominal assignment, for in Honolulu little art was exported, but quite a lot was smuggled in. She excelled at chasing down smugglers, and her "recovery rate"—an important measure—was higher than most of her colleagues'. Leilani knew the shadowy world in which she worked, and knew how to turn it to her advantage.

In her, the races mixed richly. She was thirty-three, with warm bronze skin, long straight black hair, high cheekbones, and wide dark eyes with thick lashes. Her nose was small and fine, and her lips were full. She was dressed in an orange silk blouse and a beige linen skirt; a necklace of expensive pukka shells was her only jewelry. Except for a light lipstick, she wore no makeup, and her hair fell free about her shoulders. A casual observer would take her to be a well-to-do Hawaiian housewife or mistress, an impression she sought to emphasize, since it made it easier to go about her business.

At Pearl City Tavern she ordered a fresh fruit salad and coffee, and though she was annoyed that the fruit turned out to be canned, she was not surprised. It required a very special logic to serve imported canned fruit when the real thing could be plucked out of the fields a few miles away. Leilani was barely ten minutes from Pearl Harbor, twenty minutes from Honolulu, and two minutes from a pineapple plantation, but she might have been in another country. The tavern's decor seemed to be a failed attempt at a tropical look. As she watched the long-tailed monkeys in the glass cage behind the bar, she tried to determine what it was about this place that offended her. The restaurant, with its big cage of tedious little animals chewing fleas off of one another, its aquariums, the taxidermy on its walls, was a popular hangout in Pearl City, a town full of Navy people and locals, an uneasy mix that sometimes erupted into violence. It began, as often as not, with too many drinks at the Pearl City Tavern.

Toshiro's Pet Shoppe was a mile away down Kam Highway toward Pearl Harbor, tucked away inside a shabbily built shopping center patronized by people without enough money to go elsewhere. Toshiro's apparent business was goldfish, koi, and local animals and the paraphernalia to go with them. On islands where animals roam free, where the air is full of exotic birds and there are strict rules of quarantine to protect the precarious environment, a pet shop is a fairly unusual enterprise, unusual enough to come to the attention of the United States Customs Office. Leilani, one of nine special agents in the islands—two of whom were women—had been told to check out Toshiro, and she knew she had come up with a winner.

Roger Chow, a garrulous Chinese, and Carl Spelling, the office lothario, were the other special agents dispatched to assist Leilani in handling the owner and the contraband in Toshiro's Pet Shoppe. They had walked into the restaurant while she was still picking at her fruit salad. Both were capable agents, and she worked well with them. She also made sure things remained businesslike—especially with Spelling.

"I'll take him," she told them. "Roger, you take the back of the store. Somebody may be back there, and I know there are birds. Spelling, you back me up."

"Anytime," Spelling said with a grin.

She ignored him. Normally, she would have deferred to the men. That was the way it worked in the office—they were both senior to her, and Leilani was an observer of custom—but this was her project, and Toshiro had offended her. She wanted to arrest him herself.

She felt a slight shudder of nervous apprehension as they

walked toward the shop. She breathed deeply, trapping her composure before it could escape. She was carrying a large purse made of brown leather, which was open at the top. She carried it casually over her left arm. In this position it was easy for her to reach over quickly with her right hand and pull the two-inch Detective Special out of the compartment sewn into the side of the bag. She didn't like carrying it, but the rules specified she be armed whenever she was on duty. She was also uncomfortably aware that more Honolulu agents had been shot in the last year trying to stop the smuggling of rare animals than had been shot by dope smugglers. She had had occasion to use the gun, but always as a threat—and she had never fired it except at the mandatory monthly target practice.

"Change your mind?" Toshiro said as he looked up and grinned at her. His smile turned to slackjawed surprise when he saw the two men with her. Spelling, the most benign-looking of men, pulled out a pistol while Leilani flipped open her wallet. Toshiro looked stunned.

"United States Customs. You're under arrest," she said.

"Shit." He raised his hands into the air, and as he did a look of absolute panic crossed his face. His terrified gaze was not on the agents, but on the door leading to the rear of the shop.

Roger Chow quickly slammed through the door, sending up a startled screech from the birds. "It's clear," he yelled back at them.

Leilani walked to the cage. The lorry was still there. She walked quickly toward Roger. Chow was on his haunches, peering into another cage. "There's one in here, too," he smiled up at her. Within three minutes they had been through the shop, and the count of Tahitian lorries remained at two. It was a substantial discovery.

"Don't forget to check the reptile cages," Spelling called as he handcuffed Toshiro. Leilani and Chow quickly looked around. She found only three snakes, all harmless and not one of them illegal. It confounded and infuriated her whenever she thought of it, but the reality was that a huge market existed in the United States mainland for smuggled reptiles—snakes in particular—and Honolulu was one of the major ports of entry.

Leilani took a small empty cage from a shelf and began trapping the lorries. When she had them both, she set the cage on the counter in front of Toshiro.

"These are the blue birds I was looking for," she said to him. He glared at her but did not respond.

"Is there a Mrs. Toshiro?"

"Yes."

"Would you like to call her to come here before we take you downtown?" Leilani asked him. She was being kind, though she doubted he was aware of it. She was concerned the animals would not be fed if he ended up spending a night or two in jail. She was quite sure he would have bail money—his kind usually did—but she also didn't want to leave the animals untended.

Spelling drew his gun again, unlocked Toshiro's handcuffs, and handed him the telephone. He dialed, spoke briefly, then his voice went up several octaves and he put down the phone with a loud crash. Chow picked it up from the floor.

"I don't think Mrs. Toshiro agrees with some of her husband's business practices," Chow, who understood some Japanese, said to his partners. "Let's go, Mr. Toshiro."

As Spelling escorted the furious, waddling owner from the store, Leilani turned to look around the shop and decided to check the back room again. Chow was searching the drawers of the counter and the cash register.

In back was a small, enclosed area lined with shelves of cages. There was a small toilet, a workbench, and a sink. The only sound was the dripping faucet. Near the sink, connected by a hose to a filtering system, was a large import tank of koi, and the big gold-and-yellow fish were swimming idly. Then she noticed three dead koi on the bottom of the tank.

As she walked over to the tank for a closer look, her foot hit a wastebasket beside the workbench. She looked down at it and could see the tail of another dead koi hanging out of a wad of *Honolulu Bulletin* want ads. Then she saw a used prophylactic lying obscenely to the side of the dead fish.

She reached for the fishnet sitting next to the tank. She dipped it in and pulled out one of the dead koi. She dropped the fish in the sink and it landed belly up. Its belly had been cut open and sewn shut.

She grabbed a pair of scissors and started to work. The fish, about eight inches long, had been dead for some time, and its skin was already deteriorating. Inside it, she saw the knotted end of a rubber. She pulled it out.

The rubber contained a tightly wrapped package. She was certain it would be heroin or cocaine. She was astonished to find instead four small jade insects: cicadas, in several colors, two of them almost translucent.

They were magnificent. Leilani knew that she was looking at something very valuable. She turned the insects over and inspected them. Her informed guess was that they were very old, probably predated the birth of Christ. She also knew that there was more jade sewn into the bellies of the two fish still lying at the bottom of the tank.

"Kapu, kapu," she muttered to herself as she slit open another fish. *Sacred.*

3

Jeffrey felt like an insider. No, a semi-insider. One-foot-in-the-door type, he thought to himself as he braced against the cold and set out on the short walk from the Ritz Carlton. What made him feel like a semi-insider was that he was walking without a map. He had consulted it carefully before he left the hotel, then decided he knew his way well enough.

Washington is a deceptive city. L'Enfant created a place of great broad avenues intersecting circles, with streets radiating off the circles. The result is a sort of open-ended elegance. Yet anyone accustomed to conventional city-style square blocks is in for a disorienting surprise. Jeffrey likened the city's layout to the country's foreign policy: perplexing at best.

He was dressed in a black pin-striped suit he had bought at Hackett's on Kings Road in London, a Turnbull and Asser shirt, and the tie from Britches. This, he thought, made him perfectly diplomatic-looking. It had been years since he'd owned a top-coat, so outside he looked like most Washingtonians braving the wind and cold—bundled in his lined Burberry, a scarf wrapped around his neck.

After a brisk ten-minute walk, he found himself at the Singapore embassy's chancery, a building dedicated to business—

visas, import licenses, and anything else anyone needed to participate in the economic boom of the tiny island nation.

This had happened to Jeffrey before. Most Washington guidebooks tend to list chanceries rather than the embassies themselves. Massachusetts Avenue is Embassy Row, yet many more are scattered around the city. The guidebooks choose chanceries over embassies because most tourists are in search of visas, not ambassadors.

One rainy afternoon, map firmly in hand, Jeffrey had set out to walk to the Soviet embassy—at 1825 Phelps NW, according to his guidebook. Easy. Had he been looking to apply for a visa to the USSR, this would have been the place. It was definitely not the embassy. It was a big, old mansion converted into office space, with instructions both in Russian and English on where and at what time to line up. There were closed-circuit cameras trained on nearly every inch of the building, the latest in American technology purchased—and debugged—by the USSR.

He had found the real embassy a week later. Then he had found still another. The actual embassy proved to be a regal-looking building on Sixteenth Street, just a few blocks from the White House, wedged between the elite University Club and the headquarters of National Public Radio. It was built as a monument to the tsars, and from the street Jeffrey could see a commanding portrait of Lenin staring down at the masses from the landing atop the grand staircase. Between the embassy and the University Club was a short alley which, in a fit of pique, the host city had renamed Sakharov Lane.

Jeffrey had been intrigued to find out that the embassy situation—at least the Soviet predicament—was even more complicated. The Russians had built a new embassy on the top of Mt. Alto near the National Cathedral, a massive white structure, as cold and institutional as possible in an institutional city. The huge embassy was surrounded by living quarters occupied by the Russians, but the embassy itself, now complete, remained completely empty. When the Americans discovered the bugs in Moscow, they told the Russians they couldn't have their new Washington building until all the bugs in the Moscow building were exterminated. That process was taking years.

On the cold night he walked up to the door of the Singapore chancery, Jeffrey knew for certain he was in the right place. This was the address on the invitation. And he could see the reception line of dark-suited Asian men and beautiful women dressed in the airlines' Pierre Balmain sheaths, the women Singapore Airlines advertised as "Our Girl, the Heart of Singapore Airlines." Jeffrey walked to the door, stepped inside, and shed his coat and—temporarily—all the consciousness-raising about women's rights that Rachel had imposed on him over seven years. He simply could not think of the beautiful young women as the heart of anything. He was struck by their other parts.

One of them—no doubt trained to do just as she did—picked up on his lusting look, introduced herself, and steered him into the big reception room adorned with photos of beautiful women, big 747s, and exotic destinations. As quickly as she intercepted him, she left him standing alone at the bar.

He ordered Singaporean beer, found it was delicious, and looked about the room. There were Oriental and Indian stewardesses everywhere, many of them offering trays of hors d'oeuvres.

"The only way to fly," Jeffrey muttered to himself.

"Yeah, but try getting near one of them," the man next to him answered. Jeffrey smiled and moved off, cloaked in the comfort of his ego. He was convinced he could if he really wanted to.

Except for the beautiful hostesses and the delicious Singaporean beer and hors d'oeuvres, however, Jeffrey's first diplomatic function was looking like a bit of a bust. There were no great intrigues to be seen, no pomp, no ceremony, just a lot of what experienced journalists referred to cynically as "pouring the way to progress": You get some of these people drunk enough, they'll write anything. He was quickly bored, and finally wandered out of the big main reception room into a side room which, it turned out, was a library.

What a library. After a minute or two, Jeffrey realized that he was looking at a magnificent collection of books about Southeast Asia in general and Singapore in particular. Some, he could see, predated Raffles's arrival on the little island and the beginning of its long British domination. Jeffrey stood, hands clasped behind him, studying the books, enviously admiring the fine inlaid bookcases and shelving. It was as if he had stepped into a corner of the dismantled British empire transported to Washington, D.C. It wasn't just a library, it was a reading room, one much more suited to British gentlemen than to the scholars, students, and businessmen who used it.

"You like our library?"

"Oh, very much." Jeffrey turned, looked directly ahead, and then down into the smiling face of a short Oriental man in glasses and a dark suit, which could have come from the same tailor as Jeffrey's.

"It is one of the very best of its kind," the man said formally.

"I should think so," Jeffrey responded, trying to be as courteous as he was, at this minute, curious.

"I am C. D. Lee. I'm with the embassy."

"Jeffrey Dean," he responded quickly, then paused to correctly remember his bona fides for the party. "*Today-Tomorrow!*"

"Ah yes, the new television news show." Lee looked impressed as he shook Jeffrey's hand. "Then you have reason to be interested in a good library."

"Oh yes," Jeffrey said. "I'm also a collector and a dealer in rare books."

"You have come to the right place."

"This isn't exactly my specialty."

"Perhaps you will let me show you one of our specialties?" Jeffrey nodded. "Please."

Lee stepped to one of the bookcases, reached up, and fell far short of his goal. He looked around, found a well-polished ladder that slid on a brass track around the cases, pulled it to him, and extracted a volume.

"One of our most valuable books. Actually, not a book, but a journal. It was kept by Sir Thomas Stamford Raffles shortly after he arrived in our country in 1819."

Jeffrey looked at the journal, gently touched its fine morocco binding, and read the entry at which Lee was pointing. It had to do with the annoyance of tigers interrupting billiard games being played by Raffles's soldiers. Jeffrey read it and smiled.

"The perils of tropical country, you might say," Lee commented.

"I would certainly consider tigers a peril," Jeffrey agreed.

"Ah yes, at that time, certainly. Which is your main work, Mr. Dean, rare books or journalism?"

Jeffrey attempted to answer as accurately as possible. Books, he guessed. And when Lee inquired about what sort of books interested Jeffrey, his response was quick and ready. "Modern literature, especially detective fiction." He was relieved to find someone interesting to talk to, and even gave Lee one of his California business cards. Lee, it turned out, was passionate about British mysteries, and was even a nascent collector. Jeffrey figured Lee needed only a little direction and prompting before he would become a serious collector.

"Tell me, Mr. Dean, have you ever done any ghostwriting? I believe that is the correct term."

"You mean writing for someone else and their taking the credit?"

"Yes."

"Not intentionally," Jeffrey smiled. The irony was lost on Lee.

"Mr. Dean, I would like to suggest we meet again. It might be I could be of some . . . assistance to you. And you could be of considerable help to me. This is, after all, a business gathering, is it not?"

"Of course," Jeffrey said.

Lee extracted his wallet from his breast pocket and handed

Jeffrey a business card. The two men agreed to talk the next day. Lee escorted Jeffrey through the reception room to the marble foyer, pausing at a small, elegant display case tucked into a corner. A gallery light above it illuminated the contents.

"Do you know about jade, Mr. Dean?"

"No, not at all."

"These are from the jade museum in Singapore, which, incidentally, also has a fine library."

Jeffrey looked down and saw a carved statue of an Oriental woman, about six inches high. Her face was serene, her robes translucent. Even he could tell she was perfect.

"In Western countries gold is the great commodity. In the Orient it is most usually jade. But a value can be placed on gold. There is no possible way to place a value on jade . . . it exceeds any value. It is of the spirit."

"I see," Jeffrey said, offering his hand and taking his coat from the Singapore stewardess who had matched him to it without asking.

"I will telephone you tomorrow morning, Mr. Dean. Thank you so very much for coming to our reception this evening."

4

The birds first, Leilani decided, after Spelling and Chow had taken Toshiro downtown for booking. Leilani went directly to Honolulu Airport, to the immigration and customs office, where she sent a telex—the Tahitians were not yet on the worldwide computer linkup—to Papeete, informing them of the birds' existence and asking for confirmation and shipping orders for their return. Then she waited, wondering where the jade came from and how it got to Toshiro's shop. She had some suspicions of her own on that score.

Leilani looked up through the plate glass window into the huge beige stone-and-concrete room, with its baggage carousels and inspection counters. Though she had spent many hours, even weeks and months at a time, in the customs room, it never failed to fascinate her. She could see the customs inspectors standing in casual groups, most of them in the light blue uniforms of the customs service, but a very few—the special agents—in civilian clothes so that they could mingle unnoticed in the crowds of travelers who would fill the big room to overflowing in minutes. Leilani had never understood what was meant by a tide of humanity until she had worked at the airport, observed the ebb and flow of human beings there, sensed their impermanence and learned for herself that every wave was the same, yet somehow different. It was a sort of relentless game, the challenge to spot the few who were anxious or different, to take them aside—sometimes to one of the small inspection rooms for a strip search—and force them to reveal their contraband. Some hid it in false suitcase bottoms, others taped it to their bodies and wore suits made—usually in Hong Kong—for smuggling. Some, drug smugglers especially, often hid their contraband inside their bodies. The inspectors knew how to search very thoroughly.

She was trained to spot the unusual, and though most of her expertise was academic, she had become proficient at working the room. She could spot jewelry, endangered species, dangerous agricultural products, and especially drugs, for Honolulu was a major point of entry for drugs from Southeast Asia.

It took an hour for the Tahitians to respond, and another forty-five minutes for Leilani to get the shipping orders entered into the complicated computer system. Finally, the birds were on their way to a sanctuary in Tahiti, and Leilani left immediately for her regular office at the Federal Building in downtown Honolulu.

Roger and Spelling were waiting for her.

"The fat Jap got himself sprung in about ten minutes," Spelling informed her. He appeared not to notice Leilani's and Roger's sensitivity to his racial slurs, and used them to provoke, not offend. His partners hid their objections and refused to respond.

"Damn. I was certain he'd still be in custody."

"He has a record," Roger added. "Two smuggling convictions, sentences suspended. This guy's been around . . . and he has connections. The suspended sentences are the real giveaway."

She pulled a small towel she had taken from Toshiro's store from her purse and unwrapped it.

"Wow," Spelling said.

Chow leaned in for a closer look. "I'd say these are very, very old. What sort of bug are they?"

"Cicadas, I think."

"How'd you find them?" Roger asked.

Spelling listened in silence until she mentioned the prophylactics.

"I'd love to watch you unroll one of those rubbers." Spelling could barely hide his amusement.

"You just give it a good hard yank, Carl," she said without a second's hesitation. Roger grinned, Spelling winced, and Leilani swallowed her small smile of triumph.

The three of them worked together often. They were an unlikely team—mismatched by nature but suited perfectly by function. Roger was a third-generation American, yet also a Chinese traditionalist with strong family loyalties. He was utterly reliable and a devoted husband and father. His two sons played Little League baseball, and Roger coached both of their teams. Leilani understood him, and they had become good friends.

To Leilani and Roger, Carl Spelling was an outsider—one they accepted, but an outsider nonetheless. He was from the mainland, transferred in—after his own persistent requests—from Detroit.

He wasn't popular in the office, especially among the women. The men pretty much ignored him, except for the not infrequent rumors about his questionable behavior on the job. In an attempt to remedy this, he had been assigned to Leilani and Chow the year before.

He was very blond, with sharp Nordic features and an easy charm, and he had a reputation as a sexual athlete. He lived well, played hard, and worked even harder. Although he had only been in Honolulu for two years, he knew his way around better than most of the native agents.

Still, he also made an occasional run at Leilani. At first she thought it was just because she was there, and single herself. Propinquity. Then she had realized he truly wanted to go to bed with her. He was the sort of man who needed frequent conquests. It was not difficult for Leilani to put a man like Spelling at a disadvantage, since to him any refusal implied a conquest for the other person. Leilani won simply by refusing.

The three of them, huddled over her desk inspecting the jade insects, inevitably attracted the attention of Mark O'Brien. He walked out of his office and stopped to see what they were looking at.

"These valuable?"

"Oh yes," Leilani and Roger said at once. Spelling merely nodded.

O'Brien picked one up, looked under it, hoping to find a "Made in Taiwan" symbol or something that would allow him to dismiss them. Two years from retirement, O'Brien wasn't one to encourage problems, especially problems that interfered with his golf.

Leilani explained how she found them, and told him how old she thought they might be. "I think you better go talk to Toshiro again," he said. That reaction, at least from O'Brien, was fairly standard.

"I'd thought of that already," Leilani said. She looked at her watch. It was half past five, but if they hurried they could be at Toshiro's Pet Shoppe before it closed at six. Roger quickly found the arrest sheet on his cluttered desk and handed it to Leilani to read in the car. The three left immediately for Pearl City in Spelling's new Volvo, about which he could talk as endlessly as Roger could about baseball. Whenever anyone questioned how he'd afforded it—given the expense of getting cars to the middle of the Pacific Ocean and the size of his salary—he would shrug his shoulders and smile knowingly.

Toshiro's Pet Shoppe had a big CLOSED sign in its window, and closer inspection revealed the store was locked up tight. They drove to the outskirts of Pearl City, to a little cluster of houses at the edge of a pineapple plantation. At Toshiro's home there were carefully tended bonsai plants lining the front porch, a small garden in front of the house, and no sign of either Mr. or Mrs. Toshiro.

"Let's pack it in for the day," Spelling yawned. "I know a good Chinese restaurant. You two want to eat?"

"Why doesn't anyone ever say they've found a good Hawaiian restaurant?" Leilani asked.

"There aren't any," Roger said. Spelling laughed. Leilani

hated to agree, but it was true. What was worse, she herself was a terrible cook and considered any time spent in the kitchen wasted.

Roger declined dinner, in favor of what he said was a mandatory Little League practice. Leilani pleaded fatigue. Spelling immediately began boasting about a new hot singles bar in the Hilton Hotel complex on Waikiki Beach. There was little doubt where he would be spending his evening.

The next morning, Mark O'Brien called them into his office, closed the door, and slumped wearily in his desk chair.

"Leilani, I want you to get one of those jade bugs over to the university. See what they can tell you about them."

Leilani was ready. "They'll probably tell us the bugs—they *are* cicadas—date from the Han dynasty. Roughly 206 B.C. to 220 A.D. There's really no possible way to put a price on them. It's whatever the market will take and it'll probably take a lot."

"Wow." That was all O'Brien had to say.

"I did some research at home last night, so most of this is an educated guess. I'll still take them over to the university."

"Right." O'Brien was accustomed to Leilani's quick intelligence. "That's good." He paused. "I got a call from Washington," he said after a moment's deliberation.

A call from Washington was the password in the office for serious business, because most of the Honolulu communication with the mainland was with Los Angeles. "The word is that a big shipment of jade—all of it very good stuff with high market value—is expected soon. It began a month ago as a trickle and is now becoming a stream. It's either being smuggled out of China or taken out without the government's permission. The State Department isn't sure which, and so far the Chinese are maintaining their silence."

"Any of it identified?" Roger asked.

"No. Just that there's a lot of it."

"Where's it coming from?" Spelling interrupted.

"Singapore. Their embassy people told the State Department about it."

"Any explanation?"

"No, just a rumor . . . passed along diplomatic channels."

"Is that all we have?" Leilani appeared to want all the information she could get.

"No, that isn't all. The people from State are meeting with the Singapore embassy trying to put something together. Meanwhile, I think we may have a piece of the puzzle right here." O'Brien was twisting a pencil in his plump hands, obviously uncomfortable. "Your man Toshiro washed up early this morning on a public beach over by Ewa. It would probably have gone down as nothing more than a routine drowning, except that the first cop to get there was smart enough to notice rope burns on his ankles and wrists. The coroner hasn't done an autopsy yet, but they knocked real hard on Toshiro's chest. His lungs sound empty. And they found needle marks on his arm. They figure he was shot full of drugs, then tossed in the ocean. He didn't drown. I figure he was meant to sink. Instead he drifted. And I think he's probably connected to all this."

Leilani was certain of it.

5

He didn't want to go, but he knew he had to do it. Eddie Alvaraz III counted among his many attributes a strong sense of justice and an almost obsessive conscientiousness. He was severely miscast in the physical sense, but he was going anyway.

He turned off the Ventura Freeway at Van Nuys Boulevard and headed north—as one of his sisters who lived in the area called it, "out where Jesus lost his boots." He was driving into the hinterlands of the northern San Fernando Valley, an area of the city built as a postwar bedroom community, but for many years now a bastion of the emerging Latino middle class.

That, too, was changing. As the Asian immigrants of the eighties settled into the United States, a great many of them ended up in Los Angeles. Los Angeles, always an uneasy collection of ethnic groups, was now a cauldron of nationalities and races. The Vietnamese had taken over a whole area of the eastern side of Los Angeles along the smoggy foothills of the San Gabriel Mountains. The Japanese, who had been a presence for many, many years, had long since outgrown their section of downtown and were assimilated throughout the city's endless residential neighborhoods. The Chinese, who had been in Southern California only slightly less time than the whites, kept pretty much to Chinatown, tending to live close to their businesses. The blacks stuck largely to Watts and South Central Los Angeles, their ghetto as poor and dangerous as any in the country. Their middle class, however, lived a good life in Baldwin Hills.

The Koreans were quite another matter. They had been merely a minor presence until the Korean War. Since the 1950s, they had been spreading their community along Western Avenue until they now neatly bisected the city, just as the avenue itself began high in the Hollywood Hills and ended in the slums past downtown Los Angeles. Eddie knew the Koreans tended to be acquisitive, quiet, and insular. They were also shrewd, tough businessmen, and not all of them operated within the law. Those who didn't interested Lieutenant Eddie Alvaraz III of the Los Angeles Police Department. Particularly those who dealt in stolen art and artifacts.

The mix of Spanish and Indian blood showed clearly in Eddie Alvaraz. He was short, and those who didn't know better might think he was slightly overweight. Those who did know better—and there were quite a few—knew that his extra bulk was well-conditioned muscle. His hair was black, straight and fine, his skin olive and his eyes dark brown and watchful.

He was almost, but not quite, Eddie Alvaraz, Ph.D. All he had to do was complete his doctoral thesis and the degree would be his. He had already finished most of it, a scholarly study on the religious icons of the fifteenth-century Catholic church. It was not his favorite subject, but it was a relatively unexplored and, because he was a very smart man, he had decided it would be a perfect fit for a man brought up amid the religious Mexicans of the East LA barrio. His heritage and his education gave him a special credibility, and he knew it. So did the fact that he was one of the two members of the Los Angeles Police Department who were experts on art forgery. Eddie Alvaraz loved his job.

As it traverses from the foothills of Sherman Oaks across the San Fernando Valley, Van Nuys Boulevard reflects the peculiar nature of the valley itself. That part of the street nearest the Santa Monica Mountains begins with upscale stores and quickly becomes a wide boulevard full of lavish automobile showrooms. Eddie wanted to stop and look at the BMW convertibles—even cops have dreams—but he drove on; he wanted to be on his way back to his office downtown before the Ventura and Hollywood Freeways made the transition from crowded to jammed for the afternoon rush hour.

The old Van Nuys city hall, a replica of the downtown city hall, was now surrounded by court offices, the jail, a gigantic post office, and dozens of bail bondsmen. The Hispanic neighborhood had begun. Several blocks north of Sherman Way he saw the California Korea Bank building. He looked down at the notebook on his dashboard and checked the address. Two more blocks.

It was on the west side of the street, a nondescript shopping plaza that had once been occupied by a health club and a discount store. The empty health club remained, and so did the sign for the discount store. The rest of the small center—probably a dozen stores in all—was now Korean. Their occupation of Western Avenue was spreading into the far reaches of the Valley, and so, it seemed, was the long arm of Herman Roh.

Roh's Korean Bar-B-Que restaurant occupied a corner of the shopping center. It had once been a Shakey's Pizza Parlor, but Roh had shingled the front of the building, put a blue tile roof on it, and made it instantly Korean. Roh operated out of his two restaurants, a couple of video stores, and four beauty parlors. Now there were two jewelry stores, and that alone bore watching.

Roh had built his fortune on Korean babies, at first as part of the booming adoption market run by his brother in Seoul, finally with a factory of his own in Los Angeles. He imported the young women to work in his beauty salons, threatened and cajoled them into pregnancies by any number of men who worked for him, then put the babies out for adoption. For an enormous fee, of course. The childless Anglo couples who adopted Korean babies believed they were getting little bundles direct from Korea. They were off by one generation, but hardly anyone figured it out until Roh's wife—now his ex-wife—turned him in. Eddie Alvaraz had heard all about it, and thought he might like her if they ever met. No chance of that, though. Mrs. Roh had gone back to Korea. It was the only way her ex–old man would allow her to stay alive.

When his baby boom collapsed, Roh took to importing videotaped movies and television shows from Korea, and found a ready audience for them. This was not nearly as profitable as babies, but when Roh's style of doing business was factored in, it was still pretty good money and it was a lot less troublesome than producing babies. The tapes were all pirated—no royalties, no fees—copied in Seoul by a tape duplicator manufactured in Seoul, packed off to America in the luggage of a Korean Airlines passenger, then duplicated again in Los Angeles. Roh could breed videotapes even faster than he could breed babies.

Then came the latest Roh empire: jewelry. It, too, was manufactured in Seoul. It came to the United States on the ears, wrists, and necks—and sometimes in other parts—of the stout Korean girls who came to America seeking jobs and marriage. Once he had a hot item going, Roh would put the girls in his shops to work turning out copies.

Eddie was in the valley to check out Roh's newest jewelry store. It was a bit off Eddie's assigned turf, but then the parameters of his job had never been all that clear. His specialty was art, anything from paintings to sculpture, and he was a quick study. With jewelry it took some time. Eddie Alvaraz was probably the only cop in California who kept a jeweler's loupe in his glove compartment. It came in handy from time to time.

He was dressed in a suit and tie, an attempt to look like a serious businessman. He doubted that the attempt succeeded, since his features, his body, seemed to shout no to such clothing. He rather liked it, himself.

The store was nothing at all like most Koreatown shops, which tended to be crammed with merchandise. This one was spare, almost elegant. There was a carpet on the floor, artfully arranged jeweled flowers in the window. Even the alarm system, at which he briefly glanced, looked state of the art. Roh, Eddie figured, was upgrading his image. Probably his merchandise as well.

The saleswoman was dressed neatly, her broad Korean face noncommittal as she greeted him. Eddie looked into a display case, pretending to inspect a row of gold bracelets, each intricately woven into forms of ideograms. Then he moved on to the wristwatches.

"May I show you something?"

"Yes. Do you have Omega watches?" He had already seen them.

"Oh, yes. Many. For yourself or for someone else?"

"For me. Something with a calendar . . . one I can get wet." He figured that would be one of the most expensive watches in the tray.

It was. He asked the price.

"Four thousand six hundred dollars," she said. Her tone implied that no Mexican could afford such a thing. He noticed she had no accent.

"I'll take it," he said, enjoying the mix of surprise and skepticism on her face. He handed her a Visa card. She looked at it. "It's good. You'll check anyway," he said evenly.

It was better than good. It was an LAPD-issue credit card that Eddie used to buy merchandise he believed was fake. Getting his money back was no problem, no problem at all. The watch, he was certain, was a copy, a fairly good one, and that was against the law. As he had looked at it, he had noticed a slight irregularity in the light serrations around the numerals on the dial. That was the giveaway. Maybe looking so Mexican had been an advantage. She hadn't even bothered to show him the real thing before foisting the fake on him.

While she was checking his credit, he browsed. In a heavily locked cabinet anchored to the wall, he saw a display of four jade pieces. They looked, to him, exotic and very old. About jade he knew very little, except that it was valuable and very important among the Asians in Los Angeles.

"Would you like it wrapped, or do you want to wear it?"

"Oh, I'll wear it. Thanks. But I'd like the box also."

"Of course."

"These statues here," he purposefully did not say jade. "Are they old?"

"Very." She was busy wrapping up the box.

"How old?"

"Five hundred years or so."

"Expensive?"

"Yes." Obviously she was volunteering nothing.

"How expensive?"

"Very . . ." She glanced down at his credit card receipt. "Very expensive, Mr. Alvaraz."

"I see." Eddie removed his forty-dollar Casio and slipped on the expensive watch. Expensive-looking watch.

Back in his car, he slipped the watch off and put it in its box. Dealing with the watch was going to be easy, and Roh probably anticipated such things from time to time. You don't sell forty-six-hundred-dollar fakes and not keep a sharp attorney on retainer. Counterfeit watches weren't his usual beat, but it gave him something to justify the drive.

It was the jade he was wondering about.

6

Lee, both anxious to please and wanting to appear so, chose
the Jockey Club for dinner with Jeffrey Dean. He knew that
Dean was going back to Los Angeles the next day, and assumed
that he would want to pack. The Jockey Club would be easy
for him, right down the elevator and across the lobby of the
Ritz Carlton. The Jockey was also good—good and expensive—
and it still retained its clout from not so long ago when President
and Mrs. Reagan used to sneak away from their minders and
eat dinner there.

Lee, like many who wanted to understand Americans, also
gave credence to appearances. He believed Jeffrey to be appropriate for his proposition for several reasons. For one, he
was being well paid—Lee had checked this—to help bail out
the troubled television show. Also, his work was regarded
highly enough that he could take the job for only as long as he
wanted. Dean knew about books and literature, and he clearly
had some understanding of popular culture. After all, he
worked in television, didn't he? All that, and he was staying at
the Ritz Carlton, a hotel known for its well-to-do and important
clientele.

Lee didn't know that Jeffrey Dean was glad to be leaving,

had enjoyed his professional lark—as he thought of it—and was still amused that he'd ended up at the Ritz Carlton on a company bill while everybody else was stuck at another, far less elegant hotel.

Lee was a man of some import in his native Singapore, with a government position as a high-ranking business attaché. Infrequently, he also involved himself as a cultural attaché, but culture was not important in Singapore. Business was. Further, from time to time, he was asked to handle more sensitive matters. This he did very well, and in recent years he had become important not only for what he did, but also for what he knew. In Singapore, he was a man to be reckoned with, but in Washington, D.C., he was just another diplomat. His business activities had been duly noted by the appropriate division of the State Department, as had his cultural function on those rare times it was used. He had also been duly noted and thoroughly investigated by the CIA. In all that he did, the United States government recognized little of importance. And that was the way he wanted it.

He also wanted something from the man he could now see being led to him by the headwaiter. He noted that Dean was wearing the same pin-striped suit he had worn at the Singapore chancery party, but he also noted—now as then—that it was an expensive suit. He stood to welcome his guest.

Because he was Oriental, scrupulously polite and instinctively formal, he had planned exactly what he would say and when he would say it. First came conversation, conversation with a purpose. Lee was curious about Dean's knowledge of rare books. Over drinks—both men had chosen white wine, and only one glass of it—Lee disclosed that he had found a first edition of a favorite book at a Georgetown bookstore: Agatha Christie's 1942 novel *Five Little Pigs*. He confided he was thinking of buying it.

"What is the asking price?" Jeffrey inquired. He was actually thinking that if it was low enough he'd run by and get it on his lunch hour tomorrow.

"Four hundred dollars." Lee attempted a noncommittal smile.

"Too high, unless you really want it," Jeffrey told him. "What do you think would be Christie's most collected book?"

"I don't know."

"Probably *Ten Little Indians*. It's a classic of its form, and has a fascinating publishing history."

"And that is?" Lee was definitely interested.

"In this country it was published as *Ten Little Indians*. In Great Britain the book was called *Ten Little Niggers* when it came out in 1939. It seems that the title was too strong even for the U.S., so it was changed when it was published here in 1940."

"There were many prejudices within the British empire, all to sustain their sense of superiority," Lee said evenly. "Not just for blacks—a lot of it was directed at us Asians. But no more—at least if it does still exist, it is hidden."

"You could say the same about the empire," Jeffrey smiled. "It still is an interesting publishing history. The other, very popular book, of course, is *Murder on the Orient Express*."

"Ah, one of my favorites. The movie too, the most recent one."

"I enjoyed the movie too. And the book is a Christie classic, you're quite right. I have a copy at my store in Los Angeles. A British first. Signed by Christie."

"You do?"

"Yes, I do, unless it's been sold since I came East."

"How do you run a business in Los Angeles and work here too?"

"I seldom do both, that's the easiest way. This time I have someone working for me most days, and my"—Jeffrey could never quite figure out how to describe Rachel; she wasn't his wife, but was far more than his girlfriend, and he loathed the more popular expressions—"my lady knows my business and helps out with it quite a bit."

"How lucky for you."

Not lately, he wanted to say. Instead, he concentrated on the menu.

Both ordered salmon for dinner, Lee because he was watching his weight, Jeffrey because he was half-watching: he ordered salmon so that he could justify a chocolate soufflé for dessert. He had heard the Jockey Club's was among the best in Washington and required forty minutes to prepare.

They were drinking decaffeinated espresso and Jeffrey was spooning into his soufflé when Lee got down to business.

"Mr. Dean, you will recall that I asked if you had ever ghost-written a book?"

"I remember."

"That is what I wish to discuss with you. The prime minister of my country wishes to write a book about the economic miracle of Singapore, and he will need assistance."

"Why not somebody from Singapore?"

"That was considered but is not the best choice. The reason is that the book is to be written in English for circulation among English-speaking businessmen and politicians. My government, of course, will publish it."

"A rather expensive vanity publication."

"Vanity? I do not understand."

"In this country, when someone writes a book no real book publisher wants, they go to a vanity publisher and pay to have it published."

"Oh my, this is not that sort of thing. Its purpose is to attract even more business."

"I assumed that. But why have you chosen me?"

"Not chosen, not yet, Mr. Dean, though I will say you are my prime candidate. You know words, you know books, and you also know popular culture, popular communication, whatever you call it. That is very important."

"For a book aimed at businessmen and politicians?"

"Oh yes. And more. The book will be a part, the most significant part, of a massive campaign that will spread from commerce to tourism. We plan to print half a million copies."

"Impressive."

"Are you interested?"

"That depends on certain things."

"Money, Mr. Dean?" Lee hid his smile. He always preferred to be asked before he was forced to bring up the subject. It gave him an advantage and he knew it.

"That is one of them." Jeffrey, at heart the informal American, couldn't bring himself to address Lee as Mr., so he chose not to address him personally at all. If nothing else, this was a free dinner, no more, no less.

"I am prepared to pay you sixty thousand dollars for about two months' work, only part of which must be done in Singapore."

Jeffrey was startled and he hoped he hid it well. Before he could swallow his last bite of soufflé and think what to say next, Lee continued.

"First-class airfare, of course, and all expenses." Then Lee remembered Dean had mentioned a lady: "For two, if you wish."

"What you offer is interesting for several reasons, and I would like time to think about it."

"A week only, Mr. Dean. It is time to begin." He didn't add that the other writer the government had hired had quit at the last moment because of poor health, and that the project was already behind schedule. Schedules were of crucial importance to the Singapore government. The price had been raised to increase the rate of work. This assignment had come to Lee at the last moment. He intended to complete it and, in the bargain, get back to Singapore. He had business to do, business that had nothing to do with the government but everything to do with the power he had carefully accumulated while working as a civil servant. Lee signaled for the check.

They left the restaurant together. Jeffrey, towering over his companion, extended his hand.

"Mr. Dean. That copy of *Murder on the Orient Express* you mentioned. What year was it published?"

"Nineteen twenty-six."

"And how much is it?"

"Twelve five." Signed first editions by Christie with dust jackets intact were extremely rare. Jeffrey was certain the price would put him off.

"If you still have it, I'd like to buy it."

Jeffrey grinned as he walked back to his room. The money was very good. Even Rachel would agree with that.

7

Singapore dazzled him. It also energized him, despite the oppressive heat and jet lag from the long Pacific flight. He could barely force himself to stay in his hotel long enough to unpack. The government installed him, like some piece of prize equipment, at the Hilton International, in a suite with a bedroom, a small kitchen, a living room, and a study equipped with the latest in computer equipment and an IBM typewriter–memory system still in its plastic wrapper. Jeffrey was traveling first class, no doubt about it. The suite was wonderful. The view was spectacular.

It seemed to him he could see all of Singapore, from the lush tropical greenery punctuated with the deep red of the tiled roofs on the older buildings, to the high rises that were everywhere, many still under construction. He could even see the top of a cable car in the distance, its red cars bobbing happily along. What surprised him most was the perfect cleanliness of the place. He wondered if the entire island nation was run by Disney, and if there were neatly uniformed people scurrying about cleaning up every gum wrapper, every cardboard cup.

The last thing he did before he headed out to dinner was stack his books, a ritual performed whenever he or Rachel settled into a hotel room. The novels, paperbacks mostly, he put by his king-size bed. The reference books he had found waiting for him he lined up neatly on his desk. Agatha Christie's *Murder on the Orient Express,* with an inscription from the great lady herself, he placed—still carefully wrapped—on the entrance hall table, pushing aside the vase of fresh flowers in the process. He placed the bill for the book directly on top. For now, his relationship with C. D. Lee was strictly business, and he wanted to keep it that way. Lee had arrived ahead of Jeffrey, and had left a note saying he'd be at the hotel for breakfast.

He showered, shaved, decided against a necktie, and headed out, making no effort to hide the exuberance in his step. In the lobby he consulted his map, then walked onto Orchard Road. He turned left where the map held out the promise of the International Food Bazaar and a warren of streets that intrigued him if only because one of them was named Smith: such an ordinary name in such an exotic place.

The sidewalks were wide and spotless, and instead of the usual littered curbs, there were planters full of flowers, larger planters with trees, and between them the occasional exit onto the street itself. Then he noticed the pedestrians. They all seemed to be strolling at leisure, dressed casually but well. The men, with few exceptions, were without ties and jackets; the women were fashionably attired by comparison. And there were quite a few women, several of whom smiled at him as they passed. He assumed they were prostitutes, though he wasn't sure. No prostitutes he had ever seen were so elegant.

He smelled the International Bazaar before he saw it, and was delighted by the clean stalls, the array of food, and the small tables scattered about. He immediately joined a queue at a busy Chinese restaurant and within minutes he was standing with a full tray deciding where to sit.

Then he saw her. She wasn't Chinese, she wasn't Indian, and he was quite certain she wasn't Malay. Whatever she was, she was remarkable. It was as if she sensed her difference from all of those around her and relished it, an exotic sitting alone at a table concentrating on her meal, looking about her from time to time. Her gaze landed on Jeffrey, but it was a passing glance and he doubted she had even noticed him.

There were hardly any seats available in the crowded bazaar. This was too much of a temptation to resist. He was aware that his shirt was blotched with sweat, but he figured he wasn't the only man around to perspire in such heat. Why the hell not?

"Would you mind if I sat at your table?"

"No, please sit. I'm just finishing."

"You speak English."

"Yes. Of course." She turned back to the book she was reading, seemingly oblivious to his presence.

He began eating, and by his second bite he was inventing her for himself. She was the daughter of an English lord and a beautiful Eurasian, come together in passion during the last days of the British empire. She was educated, rich.

"My name is Jeffrey Dean," he said, extending his hand.

"Hello." She did not offer her name, but she did take his hand. Hers was cool, his was moist.

He felt some horrible cliché getting ready to rumble up out of his mind, some off-putting thing like "Do you come here often?" Instead, he said, with a trace of self-consciousness, "This is my first time in Singapore. It's quite astonishing."

"My first time, too," she said, barely looking up, and shattering all of his exotic fantasies. Where was she from?

"Where are you from?"

"The U.S.," she answered evenly. "Just like you."

He smiled, he couldn't help it. So much for his imagination. "What business are you in?"

He noticed she tensed slightly, but her loss of composure was only momentary. "I'm an importer." There was no pause, no consideration. A straight answer. "You?"

"A number of things. I'm here to work on a book for a government official."

"You're a writer?"

"Yes."

She leaned back a bit, almost as though she was relaxing for more conversation. She also looked at her watch, and then directly at him.

"It was nice talking with you." She stood up, adjusted the strap of her purse on her shoulder, and left.

"Good-bye. I hope I see you again." She couldn't have heard him, she was already three tables away and walking with great purpose. "Lots more of you. All of you in fact," he muttered to himself, then added by way of brief contrition for his fantasy: "Forgive me, Rachel. Just dreaming."

While he finished his dinner he consulted his map again, then set out to see Smith Street. Such an ordinary name, he figured, might well turn out to be an exotic street.

He was right. Smith Street proved to be one of several streets in an older section of town, and he was captivated by it. It was short, barely fifty yards long, and to walk it he had to thread his way between the open food stalls, the merchandise displays, the cages of live animals, and everywhere, the people. Some were eating, some were shopping, some simply standing and looking. All of them were talking, and the din of voices was so great that it prevailed over the shrieks of protesting chickens, which were everywhere.

This, he decided, must be the real Singapore. The buildings on the street were no more than two stories high, all of them painted in light colors or pastels, paint peeling, with window shutters in bright contrasting shades. In every other window, it seemed, a caged canary watched the procession of humanity below.

"Do you have *Playboy* to sell?"

"What?" Jeffrey looked down and saw that he was standing at a table full of magazines. The vendor, a dark, intense Chinese boy with glittering eyes and bad teeth, couldn't have been more than twelve. "*Playboy*. The magazine. Want sell one?"

"I thought you were doing the selling."

"I want buy one. You got one, mister?"

"No." Jeffrey still didn't understand, but he figured the young man wasn't about to explain. Certainly, girlie magazines couldn't be hard for a young boy to find in a neighborhood like this.

Moving on, he found himself standing about a foot from the grill of a tiny makeshift restaurant, looking into a cage of live snakes, wondering what they must taste like, when the babble was punctuated by a shout for help. A woman's voice.

A gunshot followed. The noise on the street stopped, and in the stunned silence he could hear someone running down a flight of wooden stairs. The single runner suddenly became two. Or more.

Then she burst out of the doorway directly across from him: the woman whose table he had shared only minutes before. She was no longer composed. She was running, clearly terrified. Two men were chasing her, one of them—aware he was on a public street—tucking a gun into his belt. In an instant she saw Jeffrey and ran in his direction. He started toward her, then felt a strong hand grab his arm.

"Stay out of it," a husky voice said. Jeffrey spun to his right and saw a heavily made-up woman. She grabbed his arm and pulled him to her. He tried to jerk himself away, but she tightened her grip. He wrestled himself free and when she reached for him again he shoved her hard. She crashed into the cage of snakes, sending the portable grill, the cook, and several customers sprawling. The cage door popped open, scattering snakes among the restaurant's patrons, all of whom scrambled to flee. But the woman would not give up. She grabbed him by his leg, but he kept pulling away, dragging her along with him. Then he reached down and grabbed her by the hair. Her wig came off in his hand. She grabbed for it with one hand, clinging to his shoe with the other. He stepped out of his shoe and took off.

The open charcoal grill burst into flames, creating a clear passage for Jeffrey to race after the woman fleeing around a corner, away from Smith Street.

"Quick, this way," she shouted, barely a stride ahead of him. She seemed to know the way. Within a couple of minutes, they turned onto Orchard Road. She slowed immediately and composed herself, still walking quickly. Jeffrey, covered with sweat, limped beside her.

"Why are you walking that way? Did they get you?"

"No, I lost my shoe."

She smiled. "Well, thanks. I owe you a pair of shoes."

He could hardly catch his breath. Speaking wasn't easy, and he wondered why it was so easy for her. After all, it had looked as though it was all over for her just minutes ago.

"What . . ." His chest was heaving. "What in hell was all that about?"

"That? A misunderstanding." She was walking briskly, and when she came to the Hilton, she marched straight in. He followed.

"Are you following me?"

"What?"

"I said, are you following me?"

"Hell no, lady. This is my hotel. Nobody was taking shots at me. It was you they were shooting at." He was almost shouting.

"This is my hotel too," she said evenly. She turned and started for the elevators. Then she stopped. "I suppose the least I could do is buy you a drink." She seemed remarkably indifferent and composed. He was clearly confused.

"You could begin by telling me your name."

"Leilani Martin . . . and I believe you said you were Jeffrey Dean."

"I did say I hoped I'd see you again." The blast of hotel air conditioning was making him feel suddenly dizzy.

"You did?"

"You didn't hear me."

"This conversation isn't making sense. How about that drink? You look like you could use it." No doubt about it, she was in charge.

"Yeah, I could. Lead the way."

8

She walked into the bar with the purposeful stride, while Jeffrey limped along, feeling self-conscious.

"Shouldn't I run up to my room and change shoes? At least so I'll have two on?"

"No one will notice. Take off the other one when we sit down. It'll look like you're relaxing."

The bar was called the Music Room. The carpeting was deep, overlaid with richly detailed Oriental rugs. Plump sofas and armchairs, all in dark, neutral colors, were clustered around the room. Low tables, each with a vase full of cut flowers, occupied the center of the room. On the dark-paneled walls hung prints showing British soldiers and adventurers in the Far East of long ago. The whole Music Room was so British that Jeffrey expected to hear the music of Elgar emerging from strategically placed—and no doubt Singapore-manufactured— stereo speakers. Instead, he recognized the voice of Harry Connick, Jr., singing and playing the blues as if he were a world-weary black man instead of a young, white upper-class kid. Jeffrey knew all of Connick's recordings.

Leilani sat ladylike in a wingback chair, well away from the other occupants of the room. Jeffrey took the matching chair directly opposite her, and sank into it gratefully.

"Well?"

"Well what?" She looked uncomfortable, but only for an instant. He lost the initiative almost immediately, but not to her. The waitress, a plump Oriental with a British accent, seized the moment by tidying up the table and asking for their orders. Leilani ordered tea, Jeffrey a Singapore beer.

"I want to thank you for happening along," Leilani smiled at him. "It made me feel much safer."

He wanted to say, "You should feel damn lucky I did," but he had already figured out that that sort of thing wouldn't go down well with her. Too independent for that.

"I'm glad I was there, too. What exactly was going on?"

"I figured you'd ask." She was biding her time, inventing furiously, but her confident face remained impassive. She gave nothing away.

"I figured you'd figure," he said without thinking, immediately regretting it. "I mean, I do feel some sort of explanation is in order."

"You're right. Of course." The drinks came, and she stopped, staring in some confusion as the waitress placed an entire tea setting before her, along with a plate of cucumber and tomato sandwiches.

"Oh. Oh." Leilani was confounded.

"What's the matter?"

"Would it surprise you if I said I'd never done this sort of thing before?" Leilani looked uncomfortable.

"No, it wouldn't at all. Who were they?"

"I meant the tea. I've never had all this fancy stuff before. I'm not sure what to do."

He showed her, putting the strainer in place and pouring the steaming, fragrant tea over it. She sipped, nibbled on a sandwich, and smiled.

"They don't do this sort of thing where I come from."

Jeffrey recognized the avoidance, and was even willing to go along with a few diversionary tactics. After all, there she sat, and he enjoyed watching her. But he was willing to wait just so long.

"Those two men. Who were they? And what were you doing?"

"I told you I was in the import business."

"Yes, you did. What exactly do you import?"

"A lot of things." She was stuck.

"Such as?"

"I was there to make an offer on a couple of very old jade pieces. That's all. And then those two men burst into the room with guns. They were thieves." She paused.

"And then what did you do?"

"What do you mean, what did I do? I dropped everything and ran, that's what I did."

"I see." He leaned back into his chair and crossed his leg. When his shoeless right foot came into view, he changed his mind and placed both feet back under the table. "Then you must have the jade pieces with you?"

"No. Why?"

"Why else would they chase you if it was the jade they wanted?"

"Probably wanted my money too." She knew her lie was lame, but she could think of nothing else.

"Probably." Jeffrey made no attempt to hide his skepticism.

The waitress reappeared and Jeffrey ordered another beer, and as an afterthought a couple of plates of sandwiches. "They had a lookout too."

"They did?"

"A woman. She tried to stop me from going for you. She has my shoe."

"That wasn't a woman," Leilani said evenly.

"I'm willing to swear on it."

"I saw him. I saw him hanging onto your leg. That was really a man. They call them shims here. She-hims."

"Oh come on."

Leilani laughed. "Really. Men who masquerade as women.

It's sort of a phenomenon here—I don't know why. They're really very convincing. There is a part of town where most of them go later at night, nightclubs and places like that."

"Doing what?"

"I don't know, I've never been there." Leilani was vastly relieved that the subject had switched from her to the shims, so she kept on talking, despite the fact that the subject confused and slightly embarrassed her. "The women you see walking along Orchard Road . . . most of them are shims. Shim prostitutes."

"Some customers might be in for a surprise."

"Some might prefer a surprise," she said. She had always been grateful that when she blushed her face did not color, only warmed slightly. It was almost hot now, but anything was better than talking about the jade. "Someone told me that one of the ways to tell is to look either at their feet or at the Adam's apple."

"Or somewhere else, except that it might be too late by then." Jeffrey could barely hide his amusement at her obvious discomfort. He decided that Leilani Martin was a very beautiful prude. He paused a moment to think of something more to say to discomfit her when he felt a hand touch his shoulder. He looked up and saw C. D. Lee.

"I didn't expect you until breakfast," Jeffrey said, standing quickly. He saw Lee look down at his stockinged feet, then glance quickly at the underside of the table.

"I was nearby having dinner with my wife and one of my daughters. I thought I'd stop by and see how you are doing."

"Fine. I'd like you to meet Leilani Martin. This is C. D. Lee." Lee no longer wore his statesmanlike clothing. Now he was dressed for the tropics, in khaki pants and a long shirt, perfectly pressed. Without waiting for an invitation, he sat down and ordered himself a beer.

"And what do you think of Singapore, Mr. Dean?"

"Fascinating." He decided instinctively to conduct a small test, not sure of its purpose or of what results he expected.

"Mr. Lee is with the Singapore government," he said to Leilani. Then to Lee: "Miss Martin is an importer."

"I see. And how long have you been here?"

"Just a couple of days. Sightseeing mostly." She stared at Jeffrey, willing him to say no more. "And I've planned a busy day tomorrow, so I should say good night."

"No, no, not at all. I insist you stay. I myself must leave, my family is waiting outside."

To Jeffrey she seemed obviously relieved. Lee excused himself, reminding Jeffrey that he'd see him in the morning. At eight.

"What exactly does he do with the government?" she asked when Lee was gone.

"Oh, quite a lot of things." Jeffrey was smiling.

"Such as?"

"Such as . . . I think he might be interested in what happened to you tonight."

"What for?"

"You know, I'm not sure." Jeffrey sat back and looked at her. "But I will tell you one thing. Your story—at least the one you're telling me—is what we refer to stateside as a load of bullshit. Whatever you're up to, whatever it is you're doing, I hope you survive it in good shape. I don't mind helping a pretty woman in distress, but I do mind being lied to."

She was stunned, but was too stubborn to show it. "I resent that."

"Right," Jeffrey said, standing. "I'm glad I don't have to believe it. See you around sometime. Thanks for the beers and sandwiches." Holding his shoe in his hand, he walked out of the Music Room with shoulders high, hoping he looked a little bit dignified and a lot indignant. When he left the bar, he heard the opening bars of Gershwin's "An American in Paris." It was playing in the elevator too.

He walked into his suite, turned on the lights, and flung his shoe to the floor. Then it registered. Something had changed, and he couldn't figure out what. It was subtle. He looked in the bedroom, then the kitchen. When he was back in the living room he figured it out. The flowers in the entryway, where he had put the Christie book. They were the same flowers, but they had been moved, switched with the book. Then he went back into the bedroom and looked at the stack of books he had placed at his bedside. Two of them were not in the order in which he had left them. His room had been searched. Whoever had done it, they were pros. But why?

He tried to figure it out as he started to undress for a shower. His shirt was smudged and dirty, and when he took it off he could smell the sweat of fear on his clothing and his body. He began with a bath, emptying the entire bottle of bath oil the hotel supplied, creating a cumulus of bubbles and warmth. When he was done soaking, he took a cool shower.

By the time he stepped out of the shower, his jet lag had caught up with him.

The knock startled him. He wrapped himself in a towel and cracked the door open.

"Mr. Dean?"

"Yes." He could see a slim, short Chinese man, almost undistinguishable in the shadows of the hallway.

"I came about the . . . the incident tonight. I think I can help you."

"I don't want any help."

"With respect, Mr. Dean, I think you may need it. I have a proposition for you. May I come in please? I'll only stay a moment."

Jeffrey was too tired to resist, and too curious to refuse. He opened the door and the man walked in. He was hardly inside when he turned, smiled, and appraised Jeffrey, staring at his body with a blatant interest that was both confusing and irritating.

"Excuse me while I put on some clothes."

"As you wish."

Jeffrey walked back into the bathroom. Should he shut the door to the bedroom to dress, or should he keep it open so that he could watch this man? Tired as he was, his adrenaline was keeping his head clear. He quickly donned the hotel's thick terrycloth robe and slicked back his hair.

"What incident tonight?" he asked as he walked into the sitting room.

"I have neither the time nor the inclination to play along with your misguided innocence, Mr. Dean. You know exactly what incident I mean."

The man was sitting languidly on the sofa, half turned, one leg elegantly crossed over the other. He was short and delicate. The scent of his cologne filled the room. His physical appearance struck Jeffrey almost as much as his formal—and unaccented—English.

"Very well. What is your proposition?"

"If you are here looking for information, I think I can supply what you want. Actually, I can do much more than that."

"Such as?" Jeffrey walked across the room and sat down at the small table, maintaining his distance and, he hoped, an air of indifference.

"I know what you are looking for. You and the woman."

"And that is?"

"Come now, Mr. Dean. We are wasting valuable time. I can lead you to what you want."

"For a fee."

The man smiled, then reached into his jacket for a shiny silver cigarette case. He offered one to Jeffrey, and when it was declined he extracted an expensive-looking gold cigarette lighter from another pocket. He inhaled and smiled at the same time. "Yes. Of course. For a fee."

"What sort of information do you have in mind?" Jeffrey was obviously fishing.

"You are playing a very dangerous game, Mr. Dean. People who play it have been known to—how shall I put it—disappear at the most inconvenient times."

"I'm not playing any games, Mr. . . . ."

"How. I am William Wong How."

"I am not playing any games. I was merely a passerby tonight. It had nothing to do with me."

"Nor, I assume, did meeting the woman at the food bazaar just before the incident? Were you a passerby then too?"

"Actually, yes. That's exactly what I was."

"How very coincidental."

"To my regret. Do you know what she is doing in all of this?"

"Only too well. Now we are really wasting time. Mr. Dean, you are going to need some information . . . probably very soon. You are also going to need some protection, I should imagine."

"From you?"

"Certainly not. I have people who do that for me."

"What else do you do, Mr. How?"

"I own a nightclub. A very interesting place where unusual things happen . . . things I always know about."

"I can imagine. Look, let's get this straight. You seem to have some trouble understanding me. I am not involved in this, I have no need of information, and certainly no need for protection. On the contrary. I am here at the invitation of the Singapore government. On official business."

How's surprise showed and it took a moment for him to regain his composure. He quickly stood and extended his hand.

"I shall see about that. In the interim, my offer stands. I will contact you in a day or so. Perhaps then we can conduct business together."

"I doubt it very much, Mr. How." Jeffrey opened the door, then quickly closed it behind How.

He decided that he would tell C. D. Lee about the conversation over breakfast the following morning. Then he changed his mind. It might give Lee second thoughts about the wisdom of employing him. He was still swinging back and forth on his own pendulum of indecision when, three minutes later, he fell fast asleep.

9

Eddie Alvaraz, as usual, was early. He was compulsive about punctuality, a character trait he valued and also disliked, if only because of the time he often spent sitting in his car twiddling his thumbs waiting for the appointed hour. Like most prompt people he hated wasted time. The snitch had instructed him to be at a billiard parlor on Western Avenue in Koreatown promptly at nine-thirty.

Finding someone who knew something about Roh and his jewelry stores had been unexpectedly easy. He had begun by calling one of the precinct detectives who had contacts throughout Koreatown. The detective referred him to a Korean who worked for the *Korea Times*, one who was as close to an investigative reporter as anyone on the newspaper's small, underpaid staff could be. The reporter, of course, had a cousin who knew someone who worked in one of Roh's jewelry factories. The entire search for a source took just two days. An anonymous telephone caller told Eddie the address of a billiard parlor and when to be there.

He drove north on Western, wondering again why so many Koreans operated furniture stores. It seemed as though they lined both sides of the street, offering new and used furniture. The neighborhood itself, much like the new Korean neighborhood in the San Fernando Valley, was a mix of Latinos and Southeast Asians. Eddie figured he at least would look as though he belonged, even if he didn't have the faintest idea how to play billiards.

The lights of the stores glistened on the pavement still wet from the early evening rain. Eddie pulled into a side street, parked, and looked at his watch. He was fifteen minutes early. Could be worse. Five minutes later there was a knock at his window. His backup had arrived.

Sergeant Barry was a plainclothes cop in jeans and a sweat-shirt, one of the Koreatown regulars. They had met once before.

"I'll hang back . . . get in a game or something," Barry said.

"Okay. How the hell do you play billiards, anyhow?"

"I'm not going to stand out here in the cold and try to explain in five minutes. Don't play, just talk." Barry smiled.

Eddie rarely dealt with snitches, but when he did, like most cops, he wanted a little protection nearby. Hardly anything ever happened, but when it did the cop was usually outnumbered.

Eddie walked into the billiard parlor. It was unexpectedly clean and orderly, and what smoke there was was sucked up into the ventilating system. It wasn't at all what he'd expected at a pool hall. He took his seat in the row opposite the third table, as agreed, and began watching the game in progress. He watched Barry find an opponent and rack up the balls.

"You Alvaraz?"

Eddie turned. An overweight Korean man—Eddie guessed he was in his late forties, though he looked older—sat down next to him. He was clearly frightened.

"Yeah. I'm Alvaraz."

The man did not volunteer his name. Eddie proceeded.

"Roh."

"What about him?"

"Jade. Old jade."

The man looked away and lit a cigarette "Yeah. Real old."

"Where from?"

"China. That's what I hear."

"Legal?"

"Roh? You kidding?"

"Why you talking?"

"I worked for him until a couple week ago. He fired me when I ask for raise. In his jewelry shop."

"Does the jade come through the shop?"

"Yeah. Two shipments so far. Came inside dead koi . . . big goldfish."

"Pet shop?"

"Down the street. Roh smart."

"I know that. When's the next shipment . . . and where from?" Eddie looked across the room. It wasn't hard to tell who was winning. Barry was grinning. Barry looked up and nodded, acknowledging the contact.

"In two weeks. Coming in Honolulu. By ship."

"What ship?" The snitch was unusually forthcoming, and so far had asked for nothing in return.

"Don't know. I hear Roh on his phone, then he talk to someone in office. I work just outside."

"Worked," Eddie corrected him. The man's English was more than passable, but it wasn't good enough for the right tense. "Why are you doing this?"

"Roh make it I can't get new job. He threaten me."

"Why?"

"I know a lot. I want shut-up money." He ground out one cigarette and lit another.

"And you didn't get it." This wasn't the usual snitch. Eddie's instinct told him that the guy was no criminal. He just wanted his revenge.

"No."

"What else?"

"I honored threat. That enough. No more to tell." He'd done as he'd vowed, and that was that. The man got up, put out his cigarette, and turned to face Eddie. "You arrest?"

"In time."

With that, the man walked out of the parlor, and hurried down the street. Barry put down his cue and headed for the door. He was outside waiting when Eddie left.

"Vanished. Must have gone down one of the side streets or into the alley over there," Barry pointed across the street, toward where they had parked. Eddie could see a short, narrow alley between two stores, leading to a larger alley that ran the length of the block parallel to Western Avenue. They walked together toward their cars.

"Learn anything?" Barry folded his arms against the cold. A soft, misty rain had begun falling.

"Roh's smuggling antique jade." Eddie repeated the conversation to Barry, leaving nothing out. They had crossed the street and were almost to their cars when they heard the shout. They turned and ran down the alley.

Two very stout, muscular Koreans were systematically beating the man who had, only minutes earlier, given Eddie the lowdown on Roh. His face was already bloodied and his shirt covered with vomit. One of the men had a knife. Eddie could see that he intended to use it.

"Stop! Police!" He and Barry ran toward the attackers, who split up, heading in opposite directions out of the alley. Eddie and Barry took off after them.

Eddie was fast, but not as fast as the man he was after. He could see Barry gaining on his man, so he started back to help the snitch. But he was gone—the man had clearly run for his life, afraid of both the police and his attackers.

Ten minutes later, panting and drenched with sweat, Barry returned. "The sonofabitch got away. Yours too?"

Eddie nodded. "I came back to find him. Gone."

"He's going to be one dead snitch."

10

At Lee's suggestion, Jeffrey spent his first working day in his suite, poring over the books, making notes, sketching questions, and trying to learn the history of Singapore in a single sitting. The little island republic—no larger than Cleveland—had a remarkably colorful history. He became so engrossed in the historical background that he almost neglected the material on the remarkable economic miracle that had transformed the country.

His breakfast meeting with Lee had turned out to be more of a pep talk than a meeting, an attempt by Lee to make sure that Jeffrey was truly enthusiastic about the task before him. And since Lee kept the breakfast strictly business, Jeffrey decided not to mention the late-night visit from William Wong How. Later perhaps—or perhaps not. The morning went quickly, and whenever he felt restless, he reminded himself that he was here to work and that the first check from the Singapore government had already been deposited in his bank account.

At noon, he looked out his living room window to the swimming pool two floors below. There he spotted her, eating alone again, at a table near the pool, shaded by a luxuriously green tree fern. The hot equatorial sun, shining through the fronds, dappled her in shadow. He grabbed his swimsuit and a towel. He deserved a swim after a long morning's work, didn't he?

"I'd ask to sit at your table again, but I'm not sure I'm up to the consequences."

She looked up, set down the fork with which she had been delicately picking at a fruit salad, and smiled. He thought it was a guilty smile. He was right.

"I was thinking of you this morning. Please. Sit down." She gestured to the seat opposite her. "Going for a swim?"

"Yes. To cool off."

"I don't imagine it will cool you much. I swam this morning and the water is very warm." She paused. "Look. I do feel I owe you an explanation for last night."

"You mean a different one."

"Yes. Of course."

"Be careful what you say—I have a fairly accurate built-in bullshit detector."

She laughed. "So I noticed. This time the truth. I'm leaving tomorrow and it's safe to tell you now."

He took his water glass, dumped it into the planter beside him, and filled the glass from the pitcher of iced tea on the table. Then he sat back and waited.

"I'm a U.S. Customs agent, and I'm here on business. The thing is, I'm here unofficially. The government knows I'm here, but doesn't really want to know."

"Why?"

"It has to do with China. The Singapore people don't want to cause any trouble, but they also want to find out what's going on. I figure it has more to do with Hong Kong than China— or at least with the fact that most of the big businesses leaving Hong Kong in the next couple of years are moving to Singapore."

"That isn't what I meant. Why are you here? What are you after?"

"Jade. I almost had a piece of it last night, and the information I wanted, but somebody got suspicious. I think they may have figured out what I do. I don't know. Anyhow, it isn't safe for me to poke around any further, so I'm going back to Honolulu tomorrow."

"Why jade? It seems to be everywhere here."

"Not this kind. It is very ancient, very valuable."

"And it belongs to . . . ?"

She speared a slice of orange and ate it, chewing carefully. "I think I'm getting sick of fruit salad lunches." He smiled at her, then waited for her to continue.

"It's coming out of China. We think. So do the Chinese. It's one of those delicate diplomatic things, or at least that's what I'm told. Maybe to do with the Russians, too. Everyone wants to know what's happening, but no one wants to get involved. And, of course, everyone agrees it must be stopped."

"And that's where you come in."

"No, not really. I'm supposed to find out about it and that, in turn, will allow it to be stopped."

Jeffrey smiled. "This time you pass."

"Thank you."

"I gather you're telling me because you're out of it now."

"Right."

"Good. Then so am I. I had a visitor last night, a most unusual man." He could see her antennae go up. Jeffrey gave a journalistic report of the encounter, accurate right down to the fancy cigarette case and lighter.

"And he didn't say he knew why I was here, what I've been doing."

"No. He insisted I must know all of it, every bit of it."

"And now you do."

"He said I was in some danger. You too, by implication."

"I doubt it now."

She sounded disappointed. Then, before he could stop and feel guilty about Rachel, he invited her out to dinner. At Raffles. He filled her in on its illustrious history and his sales pitch worked. She accepted.

The Elizabethan Grill at Raffles was so steeped in tradition that Jeffrey looked around to see if Rudyard Kipling himself, whose picture adorned the paneled wall in the bar, might be hovering somewhere. Certainly Noel Coward, whose picture was also there, would have approved of the way the standards were being upheld. It was British, right down to the fish knives and toast racks on the tables. Jeffrey and Leilani ordered Singapore slings, a concoction invented here at the bar, generations earlier.

"That's two," Jeffrey smiled, stuffing a paper cocktail napkin and a package of matches into his pocket. He had on a tan tropical suit, a bright pink shirt, and a striped tie.

"Two what?" She was dressed in bright orange silk, a gold necklace, and matching earrings. She looked exquisite, and she knew it. In fact, they made a striking couple, and did not go unnoticed by others in the room.

"Two bars I've been to where a famous drink was invented. The other is La Floridita in Havana, where the daiquiri was invented for Ernest Hemingway."

"Havana? You?"

"Back in my days as a journalist."

The dining room itself struck her as rather heavy-handed. He thought it was perfect. Heraldic seals adorned the darkly paneled walls, and heavy black iron chandeliers hung from the ceiling almost as if electricity had been an afterthought.

"Red wine, turtle soup, roast beef, and Yorkshire pudding." He ordered for them both at her insistence. His enthusiasm was obvious, and she tried to hide her amusement at how captivated he was.

They were contemplating the dessert menu—Leilani wishing for something chocolate and Jeffrey trying to find something typically British—when the headwaiter, a Chinese whose tuxedo was pressed as straight as the part in his full head of gray hair, approached the table.

"Miss Leilani Martin?" She nodded. "There is a telephone call for you. In the lobby."

She looked puzzled and slightly apprehensive, but refused his offer to accompany her. She was back within two minutes, her face troubled.

"Someone who said her name was Melody Lim. A shim, I think. Says she has the information I want. And your shoe. She wants us to meet her at a club on Bugis Street."

"I can do without my shoe."

"I can't do without my information."

"Which is . . . ?"

"When, and how, the next shipment of jade is arriving in Honolulu."

"What's she want for it?"

"A thousand Singapore dollars."

"You've got it?" She nodded. "You armed?"

"No. Not allowed outside the U.S."

"Then I'm coming with you."

"I don't think that would be a good idea. I can take care of myself."

"So I noticed. I'm coming anyway."

She tried to dismiss him, just as he dismissed her offer to pay half of the dinner check. He was successful. She was not.

"Better lace up your shoes tight," she smiled as they climbed into one of Singapore's ubiquitous taxis.

"You expecting trouble?"

"No, not really. We'll be in a nightclub full of people."

"Good, because I'm wearing loafers again."

When they walked onto Bugis Street just after ten o'clock, it was brightly lit by neon marquees and jammed with people. It seemed an almost continuous row of bars, all advertising revues and shows, nudity and forbidden pleasures, each with a barker at the door promising great delights inside. Most of the buildings were two stories, and all had windows facing on the street. Inside, Jeffrey and Leilani could see shims wearing every imaginable costume, a riotous palette of sexuality. There were also dozens of them strolling the street, smiling at the tourists, sizing up potential customers.

Chez Jay was a not very successful attempt at sophistication among the gaudy bars. It was small and intimate, with red flocked wallpaper and gold draperies. The best seats were the banquettes lining the walls beside the stage. Jeffrey and Leilani were obviously expected: they were shown to a banquette near the front.

Attempting to hide her discomfort, Leilani adjusted her skirt, clutched her purse, and sneaked a look at Jeffrey. His profile, except for a fairly large nose, was unremarkable. But there was something in his eyes as he turned to smile at her, kindness and curiosity both at once. If he was aware of the danger in what they were doing, he effectively turned it aside. Leilani could turn nothing aside. He was waiting, she was impatient. Neither was comfortable.

The show began with a drumroll and a chorus line of Oriental shims in shiny red wigs, all of them decked out in diamonds and singing—in voices that could not quite reach the soprano range—"Diamonds Are a Girl's Best Friend." A male comedian, a swarthy Indian, came on next with all the old chestnuts about the man who hired a lady who turned out to be a man.

The comedian was followed by a striptease, and like everyone else in the club, Leilani and Jeffrey watched with undisguised curiosity. The shim finally removed his bra and there was a gasp of surprise from the audience as he turned and displayed his small breasts. There was another gasp—this one of anticipation—as he turned his back to the audience and pulled off his G-string, wiggling his rear seductively before turning around to show he was wearing a pasted on G-string beneath which it was impossible to detect any bulge of male genitalia.

"My God," Leilani whispered. "And this in a country that outlawed girlie magazines."

"A very double standard," Jeffrey grinned. Now he understood why the young news vendor on Smith Street was hungrily scouting for *Playboy*.

With a flourish of drums, a grand piano was rolled on stage and a Malay in a tuxedo, his hair brilliantined and slicked down as though he were posing for a John Held drawing, took his place at the keyboard. The lights dimmed and from stage left a platinum blonde appeared, her walk and her look instantly recognizable.

"Marilyn Monroe," Jeffrey whispered, trying to convince himself she wasn't real.

"And Chinese at that." Leilani, too, was astonished at the resemblance.

It was as though an icon from another culture had been reincarnated and neatly adapted to her new environment. She began with "I Want to Be Loved by You," and her copy of Monroe was so perfect, even her "boop-boop-a-do," had an innocent, breathless quality to it. When she was done the audience erupted in applause.

"From *Some Like It Hot*," Jeffrey marveled. "Perfect."

"What do you mean?"

"She was in the film. So were Jack Lemmon and Tony Curtis—in drag." He shook his head in wonder. The show ended with another chorus line, and then the performers moved out into the audience and began inviting customers—men and women—to dance. Jeffrey and Leilani each politely refused.

The Marilyn Monroe look-alike walked out from backstage. Jeffrey looked up and saw her approaching their table.

"I saw that you liked my Marilyn," she said to them, sliding daintily into their booth. "I also do Barbra Streisand and Helen Reddy."

"Helen Reddy?" Jeffrey could barely keep from laughing. Up close, without the soft lighting, the imitation was far less convincing.

"I'm also Melody Lim and we have business to discuss." Marilyn vanished in an instant. "To business, my dears," she said as she lifted Jeffrey's beer glass in a toast.

"You have information for sale," Leilani began in a low voice, "and I have the money you want. First, the information."

"Oh no. It's like it is at the Academy Awards. The envelope first, please."

Leilani pulled a Singapore Hilton envelope from her purse.

"For Christ's sake, not here," Melody hissed at them. "Someone will see me. I'm going to leave you now. In fifteen minutes you follow me upstairs. I'm the third room on the right. Stairway's by the bathrooms." Slinking away, she nodded and smiled at the customers, her impersonation intact.

Jeffrey asked Leilani to dance, and as they came together in a slow waltz, Leilani whispered, "I'm sure she was there that night on Smith Street. In the other room."

"Which means?"

"I don't know. She's involved somehow, or more likely involved with someone who is really involved."

"That's what I think."

He held her as close as his conscience would allow, yet close enough to feel her body move easily beneath his hands. He could smell the sweet scent of her perfume, and he was aware of how tense she was.

"This bother you?" he asked, looking directly at her.

"I want to know what she's . . . he's got. Is it time yet?"

Jeffrey glanced at his watch. "Almost." "That isn't what I meant," he wanted to say, then felt guilty for thinking of flirtation, of infatuation, of all of the things he had been certain he had left behind forever when he met Rachel.

Exactly fifteen minutes later they left the dance floor and started up the stairs. Leilani insisted on going first. Jeffrey looked around to see if anyone noticed their exit. Several shims were watching, but Jeffrey figured they probably thought he and Leilani were on their way to some sort of kinky encounter.

The stairway was wide, and so was the long carpeted hallway, lined with doors and lit by flickering light bulbs in sconces.

"As these places go, this is pretty high-class," Jeffrey whispered.

"You that familiar with them?"

It was impossible to see his blush in the semidarkness. The third room on the right had a star on the door. Leilani knocked. There was no reply, so she knocked again. Finally, Jeffrey reached around her and tried the door handle. It opened easily.

They stepped into an imitation Victorian parlor, with two

plush chairs and an uncomfortable-looking sofa. There were photographs of Melody on the wall both as Marilyn and as herself.

"Miss Lim?" Leilani paused before a partly open door. She turned to Jeffrey and whispered, "I think we've been stood up."

Jeffrey opened the door and stepped through into a gaudily decorated bedroom. Melody Lim was on the bed, her legs obscenely parted, her throat cut. Blood covered the pillow, and stained the blond Marilyn Monroe wig, which had been dislodged from her head.

"Jesus." In a misguided instinct of chivalry, he turned to block Leilani from coming in. It was too late. She stood there, looking up: reflected in the large ceiling mirror was what he had seen firsthand.

Leilani turned pale, clutched a fist to her mouth, and ran to the little gold sink on the wall. She was violently ill. Jeffrey grabbed a monogrammed towel and handed it to her, resting his hand on her shoulder. She shook off his hand.

"I'll be all right. Look . . . look around and see if you find anything." She wet the towel and wiped her face, and with a remarkable display of composure, Leilani began systematically searching the room.

In a paper sack by the dressing table, she found his shoe and handed it to him. They found nothing else until Jeffrey prodded the bedding surrounding the body. He heard the crinkle of paper, as he gently prodded the pillow on which her head rested. He reached under the pillow and pulled out a small package.

Pinned to it was the shipping schedule from the Singapore Times dated two days previously. It had been neatly trimmed from the newspaper and the name of one ship, the *Marara,* had been circled in eyebrow pencil. In the package, wrapped in the remnants of the newspaper, was a tiny, delicately carved piece of jade.

They had no sooner glanced at the jade when a great, piercing shriek filled the room. They turned to find a terrified shim in a bright orange wig standing in the doorway wearing a spangled top and holding his sequined skirt in his hand. The scream brought other partially dressed shims running into the room. Jeffrey felt as if he had suddenly been dropped into some obscene nightmare. Leilani looked for an escape but quickly realized they were trapped.

"Fast—put the jade in your purse. I've got the clipping," Jeffrey whispered. Leilani stuffed the wrapped carving in a small compartment in her purse, then changed her mind and slid it into a small pocket in her skirt.

Within minutes Chez Jay had been emptied of customers, and the upstairs was filled with police.

11

Once again he was driving up Western Avenue, past the massage parlors, markets, furniture stores, travel agents, and all the other small Korean businesses that spoke of ambition and a desire to appear as American as possible.

Sergeant Barry was waiting for him in an unmarked car well to the rear of the McDonald's parking lot.

"Thanks for the call," Eddie said, shaking the man's hand and noticing that he was once again in jeans and sweatshirt, while Eddie wore his downtown cop uniform: nondescript suit and unobtrusive tie.

"Well, it's progress, anyway. The snitch's name is Owh. O-W-H. I say 'is' because I'm presuming he's still alive. That's what his old lady tells me anyway. Hop in, I'll drive."

Barry knew the neighborhood, and they cut through the side streets to Lemon Grove Avenue within minutes. Eddie doubted there was a lemon grove within fifty miles. The past wasn't for preserving in Los Angeles—it was hardly for remembering. He turned his attention to the addresses.

The place they were looking for was an old-style stucco Hollywood apartment building, a relic from the thirties that looked considerably older. Now it was occupied exclusively by Koreans. Barry consulted his notebook and they punched the elevator button. Broken. Barry cursed slum landlords as they walked the three floors up to the apartment of Mr. and Mrs. Owh.

After a clatter of latches and locks, the door opened to reveal a round, gray-haired woman, clearly one for whom life hadn't been easy. They already knew she worked in a sweatshop, sewing her life away in the garment district. She was clearly not pleased at the prospect of a visit from the police. Still, she was a dutiful Korean wife, and she did as her husband told her to do.

"You police?"

"Yes, ma'am." Barry seemed unaware he was doing a wonderful imitation of Joe Friday.

"Here," she said, handing them an envelope. "My husband said give you this."

Eddie opened it. Inside were copies of three import bills of lading. They showed what Korean products were being shipped—television sets mostly—and on what vessels. Eddie scanned their names.

"Did he tell you anything else?" he asked her.

"Nothing. Tell me nothing. Mail me this."

"Do you have any idea where he is?"

Tears welled in her eyes. She shook her head and fumbled in her apron pocket for a tissue.

"Why is he doing this, Mrs. Owh?" Eddie asked gently.

"Because now Herman Roh makes trouble for our son. He's good boy. We obey law."

"What is he doing to your son?" Barry lowered his voice to a whisper. Sons are sacred to Koreans, and one spoke of their problems with great discretion.

"He threaten my boy. No more work. Break his legs if he doesn't tell where husband is."

"Does he know? Do you know?" Eddie asked quickly, and she gave a shake of her head just as quickly.

"Both hiding now," she said, no longer able to hide her tears.

"Did he threaten you?" Eddie finally asked her.

"Me?" She seemed surprised. "No. Korean wife not important. Never told anything. That's what Roh thinks. But we just a little bit American now." She gave a rueful smile.

Both Eddie and Barry gave her telephone numbers to call in case of trouble, and though she hardly seemed reassured, she nevertheless placed the two cards neatly by her telephone.

"She's got guts too," Barry said as he drove back to McDonald's. "Must run in the family. I'll put some heat on Herman Roh. What do you do now?"

"Find out about these ships. Where they are, when they're due."

He had his answers the following morning. All three ships were owned by a shipping company called TransPac, headquartered in Honolulu. Two of the freighters, the *Mauana* and the *Maori,* had already completed their voyages. Within the last week one had arrived in San Francisco, the other in Honolulu. Both had sailed from Japan. The third, the *Marara,* had just set sail from Singapore bound for San Francisco with a short stop in Honolulu. It was due to arrive in Hawaii in two days.

He sent immediate inquiries to the Honolulu Police Department and to U.S. Customs. He also tapped into his computer an inquiry about TransPac to the LAPD research library. Then he sat back and waited.

12

A tropical storm descended on Singapore, its clouds dark and threatening, its rain heavy and seemingly unending. The humidity, already high, now soared. Leilani, used to the storms of Hawaii, barely noticed it. Jeffrey, unaccustomed to such beautiful and nourishing violence in nature, felt threatened. It was just one more disturbance on top of a heap of disturbances over which he had no control at all.

He and Leilani were sitting on a marble bench outside a government official's office, this one a good bit more impressive than the others they had encountered in their crash course in the Singapore justice system. They knew they were somewhere in a Singaporean limbo between the police, the foreign office, and probably someplace else as well—but just where was unclear to both of them. They had been up all night. Now it was morning and they were waiting, guarded by a police officer, for office hours to begin, for the official—a Mr. Chen—to appear and begin his daily duties.

From Melody Lim's boudoir on Bugis Street they had been escorted—after a flurry of radio communications between the police and headquarters—back to the Hilton Hotel. There, they were escorted separately to their rooms, where they surrendered their passports. Finally, they were taken to individual holding cells, where they were informed they would be spending the night. Both Leilani and Jeffrey objected forcefully but without success. Finally, they were told they would be able to call the American embassy the following morning.

They were still waiting to call when they were escorted into the well-appointed office of Mr. Chen who, it turned out, was the official charged with dealing with miscreant foreign visitors to Singapore. He greeted them formally, invited them to sit, and then dropped his bomb.

"Your passports will be retained by this office until our investigation into the murder is complete. You are free to move about Singapore, but you cannot leave." Before their surprise, their lack of sleep, and their sense of outrage could galvanize them into a reply, Chen handed each of them his business card.

"Here is how you can reach me. I suggest when you contact your embassy that you also give them my number."

"Are you saying we're suspects?" Jeffrey finally had found his voice.

"Well, Mr. Dean, what are we to think? Of course you're suspects. It is very reasonable, according to the initial police reports. You, I gather, knew Miss Lim. Your shoe was in her room . . . not one you were wearing at the time . . . of the murder."

"I can explain that," Jeffrey said, realizing that the explanation would only complicate the problem. Leilani shot him a warning glance.

"You will have ample opportunity to do so," Chen said, clearly uninterested in whatever Jeffrey might have to say. "I suggest for now you return to your hotel and rest. I'll have you driven there." He pushed a button beside his desk, the guard reappeared instantly, and Chen stood, dismissing his reluctant visitors.

"That goddamn shoe," Jeffrey muttered as they were being driven back to the Hilton.

"Shh." Leilani wasn't taking any chances. They did not speak again until they were back in the Hilton lobby, alone.

"They probably think I'm one of her customers," Jeffrey said. "What the hell do we do now?"

"We go to our rooms, shower, and rest for an hour or so, then we're going to the embassy. We'll be out of here in no time." She paused, as if to convince herself. "I'm sure of it."

What he wanted to say was, "You'd better be. You got me into this." But what he said—wearily—was, "Okay. I'll call Lee and get him on it too."

He didn't have to call Lee. He was just getting out of the shower when his telephone rang. It was Lee. Jeffrey listened, checked his watch, and concluded by saying, "I'll be there within the hour." As he dressed, he thought Lee had sounded oddly formal, or at least not as friendly as his natural reserve had allowed him to become. All Jeffrey knew was that Lee said the meeting was important and concerned the work Jeffrey was doing for the government.

Or rather, no longer doing for the government. Lee came directly to the point: "Mr. Dean, we cannot have someone involved in the murder of a shim while working on a project with the prime minister of this country. I regret to say this to you, but the book no longer concerns you."

Jeffrey felt small and inconsequential. Also wronged. His immediate instinct was to fight back, to protest his innocence.

"I see. Guilty unless proven innocent. Interesting concept of justice you have here, Lee."

"Mr. Dean, there are other matters that come to bear here. We have been discussing a death, but we have not discussed a visit to your hotel room by a man who is a known criminal."

Jeffrey nearly exploded. "By God, you people are something. You hold me responsible because a man I've never seen before—or since—comes to my hotel room. What about it?" He took a breath and attempted to compose himself. "You miss nothing. But what about my privacy? What right have you to spy on me, to record everything I do, everyone I see? I gather it was you who searched my room as well."

Lee ignored him, chose not to acknowledge his anger. He proceeded calmly. "Any person associated with the prime minister must be like Caesar's wife: Not just above suspicion but seen to be above suspicion. He absolutely insists on that."

"Well, then. I guess you go for guilt by association. After all, you're the one who gave me the job." Jeffrey tried to suppress his sense of foreboding. He had hoped Lee would be an ally, at least for part of this mess. Now he knew it wasn't to be.

"Not quite. We had you well vetted before you came here. I have that on my side. Also, I have other involvements which need not concern you. We have nothing further to discuss, Mr. Dean."

"Oh yes, we do. Understand a few things: One, I do not give refunds. The money you've paid me is mine." Lee nodded his reluctant assent. "Two, I have my plane ticket, and I'm ready to leave. Get me my passport."

"You will have your passport when the investigation is complete. It shouldn't take long. The government here is very thorough and very efficient."

"And very intrusive."

"I beg your pardon?"

"I said 'And very intrusive.' "

"Think what you wish. It does prevent our being involved in scandals."

"This is not a scandal. It's murder. My problem is that I had nothing to do with it and I want that clearly understood by all of you."

Lee remained seated at his desk, unperturbed and composed. Jeffrey finally took a good look at the office itself and saw that something was wrong with it. It was a nondescript place with utilitarian furniture in an old and undistinguished building. Given the Singaporean obsession with appearances, it seemed to Jeffrey that Lee was out of place. Perhaps it was because he lived in Washington—or so he said. Even so, being important enough to live in Washington should have entitled him to the best when he was home.

"I hear what you are saying and you may be assured I want to believe what you say. Be that as it may, the damage to the book is done, and your involvement with it is over. One more thing bears upon this decision, one I'm certain you are well aware of. Certainly you are not so naïve as to assume we are not aware of Miss Martin and what she is doing here."

"She told me the government knew what she was doing, that it had been agreed for her to do it."

"That's what she says, Mr. Dean. At any rate, this business involving the jade is a very delicate matter. We must tread very lightly. You, however, have not trodden so lightly."

"I have not really trodden at all, which is where you all seem to be missing the point."

"Shoes make treads, Mr. Dean. And one of yours is involved."

There was no point in continuing. Jeffrey stood to leave, started for the door. Lee cleared his throat, uncomfortable about what he had to say next.

"The hotel informs us they need your suite. I hope you won't mind moving to another room."

Jeffrey stopped and was about to ask who would be paying for his room when his pride got the best of him: he said nothing, merely nodded and left.

Outside, the rain had stopped, the sun had reemerged intent on heating the sticky air to a boil. He decided to return to the hotel, tell Leilani what had happened, perhaps even suggest that this new trouble of his was inadvertently her doing. First, he would go back to the hotel and move to another room. Then he changed his mind. Since he was not far from the National Museum—which Leilani had told him contained one of the world's best collections of jade—he decided to go there first for a quick look.

It was a moderately maintained Victorian building set amidst the considerable rubble caused by the construction of Raffles City, and buttressed from behind by the office towers that dominated the skyline. The museum, dedicated in Queen Victoria's time, existed in large part because of two men, the How Par brothers. In their time they had been powerful businessmen, and most of their fortune had been built on Chinese medicine. They must have been the Smith Brothers of Asia, Jeffrey thought. They had also been collectors of the world's finest jade, and they had left it to the Singaporeans.

Few came to see it. The wing of the building where the jade was displayed was empty except for two unarmed guards staring idly out the barred windows. There was no air conditioning—electric fans turned lazily on the ceiling. There were tattered light green runners on an unpolished wood floor forming a forlorn path to old metal-and-glass cases filled with jade.

The jade was a revelation, an initiation into the culture of another people. He began to understand its ritual significance. The very rich and the very royal were buried with jade inserted in all nine orifices of their bodies so that they would not decay. Jade was worshipped.

He was struck by how many jade pieces were carved in the form of fish, some exotic, others neatly representational. This, according to the booklet he had picked up at the entrance, was because fish were a symbol of wealth owing to the similarity in the Chinese pronunciation of the words *yu,* "fish," and *yu,* "superfluity" or "abundance." There were also dozens of bowls, magnificent objects carved of the finest jade—fine enough to touch the lips of their Mandarin owners. Most of the objects dated back to the early 1700s, some even earlier.

Some of the pieces were clearly designed by someone with a sense of humor. Jeffrey particularly liked a finely detailed carving in lapis lazuli of Li Po, the poetic genius of the Tang dynasty, traditionally portrayed in a scholarly attitude. Not this time. Li Po had a cup in his hand and, from the expression on his face, was clearly potted.

Li Po was in one of the last cases by the exit, and as he left, Jeffrey looked up and saw that he had been alone in the museum the entire time. On his way out, he stopped at the small gift counter where an elderly Chinese woman sat smoking and reading a newspaper. She did not look up to greet him. He browsed and then settled on a small jade snuff bottle as a gift for Rachel. It was intricately carved, even down to the bone spoon that stuck delicately out of the stopper. When he paid for it, the woman neither looked at him nor removed the cigarette from her mouth.

Thus she did not see Jeffrey leave, nor notice the man who emerged from a position just out of sight of the counter and followed him out of the museum.

Jeffrey stepped into the bright sunlight, paused, and searched his pockets for his sunglasses. He was putting them on when he heard the footsteps on the gravel pathway behind him.

"Mr. Dean, it would be wise of you to walk toward that garden just to your right. To the little gazebo at its center. That way we can talk, unobserved and unheard."

Jeffrey looked quickly behind him. It was How, now dressed as an ordinary man on the street. Jeffrey could see his own reflection, the startled look on his face, in How's mirrored sunglasses. Typical gangster glasses, he thought. His first instinct was to continue on his way, ignoring How. His next thought was, what the hell? He was curious, his job had ended. He proceeded toward the small garden and the gazebo.

"That was very wise of you, Mr. Dean. I saw your hesitation and I did not want to use force to get you to listen to me." How sat down, striking his old languid pose again on the hard wooden bench. A fountain splashed serenely in the center of the small pond by the gazebo. "Water provides a most interesting shield against interlopers," he said, turning to smile at Jeffrey.

"The jade, Mr. Dean. I want you to tell me what you know about the jade."

"Only what I know from Miss Martin."

"And that is?"

Should he refuse to talk, lie, or tell the truth? He decided to lie, but How forestalled him. "I will know if you are telling the truth, Mr. Dean. Believe me, I will know. And you do not want to know about the consequences of lying."

Jeffrey told him about the jade, knowing he sounded vague, exactly as it had been told to him by Leilani.

"Remarkable woman, Miss Martin. That is all she told you?"

"Yes."

"Strange, but I think you might be telling the truth. But certain things do not ring true. The shim, Melody Lim. She had your shoe, and I suspect she had more of you than your shoe."

"You're suggesting I . . ."

"Fucked her, Mr. Dean. That's what many men—Westerners especially—love to do with shims."

"No, I did not. I had never seen her until I saw her perform as Marilyn Monroe. I was having dinner with Miss Martin when she received a phone call saying Melody Lim had information for sale. That simple."

"No, not really. I assume the dinner you refer to was the one at Raffles."

Jeffrey's breath practically went out of him. "Jesus, between you and the government here there are no secrets, are there?"

"Only the secrets we keep from one another, Mr. Dean. I gather by the government you're referring to Mr. Lee, the diplomat."

"Mr. Lee refers to you as a criminal."

How laughed, and then paused to consider his response. He lit a cigarette with his expensive lighter. "It is hard to say who are the real criminals here, the men in the pin-striped suits or men like me."

"It's a matter of degree," Jeffrey responded immediately. "They may be criminals to some, but about people like you there seems to be little doubt."

How stood and looked directly at Jeffrey. He could see his reflection in How's glasses, and he did not like the fear he saw.

"Be careful, Mr. Dean. You are on very, very thin ice. Odd expression for such a warm tropical place, isn't it?"

With that, he walked away. Jeffrey waited a moment, then walked to Orchard Road and turned in the direction of the Hilton.

He knew he was being used, but by whom he was not at all certain. He tried to comfort himself by counting his allies, but that was even more disconcerting.

13

Eddie liked the stewardess. Flight attendant, he corrected himself. She was about his age and his height, and seemed to possess his attitude as well: She tolerated people, she wasn't all that fond of them, and she hid it well. The plane wasn't crowded, and he had the relative luxury of three seats and a window to himself—though there was nothing to see and he wasn't tired enough to stretch out. So he struck up a conversation with her.

He had been right. She shrugged her shoulders, smiled, and described the passengers on her Honolulu runs as "the newlywed and the nearly dead." She preferred, she said, to work first class. Nevertheless, she seemed to have no major objections to working the back of the plane either—or as she called it, "reheating the Alpo."

"You don't look like you're off on a vacation," she said to him.

"I'm not." He wondered how much to reveal, an especially difficult decision for Eddie, who was not at all the forthcoming sort. "I'm on business."

She pressed him.

"I'm on business for the International Federation of Art Research." It was the truth, or as much of it as he was willing to dispense.

"Really? You don't look like the artistic type. What are you doing for them?" She sat down on the aisle seat, turning to face him. Beneath her slightly hard-edged manner, he sensed immediately that she was vulnerable.

"I'm investigating some jade . . . which appears to have been stolen from China and is being smuggled into the United States." He wanted to impress her, and it worked.

"Fascinating," she said, and meant it. Then she was off to sell liquor to a group of noisy tourists. A while later the plane began its long descent into Honolulu, and land was at last in sight. Eddie looked out his window as the jet rumbled over Pearl Harbor and into Honolulu airport.

He had told the flight attendant the truth. He had come to Honolulu in his capacity as the West Coast expert for the International Foundation for Art Research, the rather lofty title attached to an organization composed of representatives such as himself from a number of nations. Their goal was to recover stolen art or, better still, to intercept it before it disappeared forever.

Eddie's investigation first into the freighter *Marara* and then its corporate parent TransPac had provoked his curiosity and, finally, had awakened the instinct that made him good at what he did. What struck him was that the president—and majority stockholder—in TransPac was a man named Alfred Davidson.

TransPac was having financial trouble—no great news in that—and Davidson appeared to be struggling to get his business back in the black, a business that had been in his family for four generations.

That alone was not enough. Yet as Eddie scanned the microfilm index one rainy afternoon at the Parker Center in downtown Los Angeles, something unusual had turned up. He had requested all references in the Honolulu newspapers to TransPac and to Davidson and the librarian had provided them—including a social note.

The society column from a year ago concerned an art exhibit cum fund-raiser held at a Honolulu gallery owned by Davidson, who, it appeared, was an art patron and collector. The gallery was called, appropriately enough, Pacific Gallery, and the show had been of paintings by two Asian artists. The fund-raiser had been the auction of several pieces of antique jade from Davidson's collection. The event had taken place the year before, yet Eddie suspected it was probably an annual affair. If so, it was about due to take place again.

Eddie had checked with his superiors, telephoned the IFAR headquarters in New York, and, temporarily setting aside his LAPD badge but not his experience, had departed for Honolulu.

Now, as he waited at the jammed luggage carousel for his single suitcase, he was startled to be tapped on the shoulder.

"Stay out of the sun. It can burn." It was the flight attendant, on her way out of the airport with the rest of the crew.

Eddie smiled. "I'm Mexican. We don't burn."

"So I noticed," she said as she walked away. He shrugged, attracted to her but unwilling to do anything about it. When Eddie was on business, he was all business.

His hotel was the Holiday Inn on Waikiki, recommended by the customs agent he had tracked down with the help of the Honolulu Police Department. He had showered, shaved, and put on a clean shirt by the time he met Spelling for a drink in the hotel lobby. Spelling turned out to be tall, blond, and, as far as Eddie was concerned, bland. He appeared interested in the jade only in an offhand way. As if to explain his disinterest, he had informed Eddie that one of his partners was away on assignment in Singapore, the other on a short leave.

"So I hope you'll excuse us if we don't seem as available as you'd like," Spelling said, looking away from Eddie at a group of three women sitting expectantly together at the bar. He didn't really seem to give a damn about Eddie's long journey—or, indeed, the purpose of his visit. Eddie hid his irritation.

Nevertheless, Spelling had done his homework. He came with more information on TransPac and docking particulars on the *Marara,* which was due in Pearl Harbor in just two days. It was carrying a huge shipment of Hong Kong–manufactured clothing and appliances, most of it destined to be distributed about the various government PXs and some discount clothing stores on the island. Within hours, the *Marara* was to be reloaded with household goods belonging to servicemen and their families. Then, it was off to San Francisco.

"Anything on Alfred Davidson?" Eddie asked after he had skimmed the material.

"Nothing at all. Old Honolulu money, his great-great-grand-father was a missionary, and his great-grandfather started the family business. Married twice. Currently divorced. Interested in art. That's all I could find."

"Anything about his jade collection?"

"Never heard of it."

They talked several more minutes, exchanging information about their work, Eddie answering a number of questions about IFAR, and his job with the LAPD.

"You armed?" Spelling asked casually.

"No. Not allowed on this sort of thing."

"They'll probably ask."

"Who?"

"My people or the police—they know you're here since I've been getting information for you. What do you have planned for tomorrow?"

"A visit to his art gallery, a few things like that."

Spelling nodded, then made his excuses. He promised to check with Eddie the following afternoon. He paid for the drinks and was about to leave, and as he extended his hand he smiled easily and said, "Oh, one more thing. Another agent—her name is Leilani Martin—has been in Singapore looking into this jade thing. She'll be back here later tonight. You can talk with her tomorrow if she comes into the office."

Eddie wrote down her name in his notebook. Then he ordered another drink and considered going for a walk around Waikiki, but decided to read Spelling's files first. He was sitting in the chair, sipping his beer, when there was a familiar tap on his shoulder.

"Are you following me?" There she was again, no longer in uniform. She was wearing snug-fitting jeans, sandals, and a silk blouse. She had a sweater draped over her shoulders.

"No. But it's not a bad idea. Actually, I was going to ask you to have a drink with me."

"You mean you're willing to stop detecting and relax?"

"Absolutely."

She sat down. Her name was Diane, she was recently divorced, had two children. One of them was in college, the other finishing high school. She had gone back to flying six years ago. He revealed as little as possible about himself. Half an hour later he put his files in his room and they walked out of the hotel to a restaurant she had heard about.

So much for "strictly business." There had to be exceptions, he told himself.

The next morning he was a very happy man. He was even a little bit in love.

14

"Wow! Incredible!" Jeffrey was dripping wet. He had been for his first swim in the China Sea, and now he was climbing like a kid over the remains of a concrete bunker the British had built facing the China Sea. It had been built to intercept the expected Japanese invasion by sea, but the Japanese had swarmed in from the other direction, striking down the Malay Peninsula. The bunkers, in the end, had been useless.

That they were still there fascinated Jeffrey. It also helped him to keep his mind off Leilani, who was wearing a bikini and lying in the sun, unaware of his lascivious thoughts and unimpressed by his enthusiasm. She had something else on her mind.

"That Chinese who came to your room. How. What were his other names?"

"William Wong How. And I've had another little conversation with him."

That got her attention.

"Why didn't you tell me?"

"His sole wisdom seemed to be that both you and I were in danger. That, I figured, was already something we knew all too well."

"Where did you see him?"

"Outside the jade museum. I stopped by to see what all the

excitement was about. Incredible stuff, really remarkable. He must have followed me."

"Jeffrey, we're not talking about jade. We're talking about How, a gangster."

"I figured the two were closely connected somehow. Here's what I learned from him in two minutes: He feels you government people—pin-stripers he called them—are just as big gangsters as his type."

With that, he was up and heading back toward the water. But that wasn't information enough for her. She decided she'd have to try again later.

They were spending a few hours on the beach on Sentosa Island, mostly as a chance to, as Jeffrey had put it, regroup. The American embassy was doing what it could to get their passports returned, but the Singapore government was not budging. They were waiting for twenty-four hours to elapse, after which the embassy official dealing with them had said the government would probably issue them new passports and see them out of the country.

After a night in jail, a good night's sleep and a day of enforced leisure was their collective wish. Besides, there wasn't much else they could do. Leilani had telephoned Mark O'Brien in Honolulu and reported to him. She made no mention of the *Marara,* choosing to let that wait until later. She was certain she'd be back in Honolulu well before its arrival.

Jeffrey had telephoned Rachel and told her everything. Her indignation over the canceled book was far greater than his, her anger more palpable. He was, she had once told him in a fit of pique, violently phlegmatic. He insisted he was not; if he never erupted as she was wont to, it was because he was just too busy planning. The weekend was coming, it was very likely he'd be out of Singapore before it, and so she had agreed to meet him in Honolulu. They'd been intending to go for at least two years, and now they had the perfect excuse for a few days alone together.

When he flopped down on his towel, Leilani peered up from

the pamphlet she was reading and said that Sentosa Island had once been named Palau Blakang Mati—she pronounced it correctly on the first try—and that the Malay translation was roughly "The Island of Leaving Death Behind."

"This was a Japanese prisoner-of-war camp during the war," she continued, paraphrasing the pamphlet she had picked up on the ferry ride from Singapore. "Then, when the government decided to develop it as a place for its citizens, a contest was held to choose a new name. 'Sentosa' in Malay means 'The Isle of Peace and Tranquillity.' Nice." She handed the pamphlet to Jeffrey.

He read for a moment. "There's a museum here, which had been an old British hospital before it became the prison camp. A museum of the occupation. Let's go see it."

"First, I swim." She was up and away, walking gracefully into the water. He watched her dive into the placid, shallow water, surface, and begin swimming. He turned back to the pamphlet and read until she returned.

"Let's go."

"Let me dry off first." She meant lie in the sun until she was dry. Jeffrey studied her surreptitiously, feeling guilt right down to the stir in his groin. I'm too young to be a dirty old man, he thought to himself, and too old to be a nosy little kid. He concentrated on the thin line of soft hair coming out of her bikini bottom and, finally, as his gaze came to rest on her breasts, he had to turn over on his stomach. That was really uncomfortable, so he scooped up a towel, covered himself, and walked to the little changing room that had been constructed out of cement blocks to complement the nearby bunkers.

They hopped on the tram for the museum and, as the guide announced in excellent English, "the surrender chamber." Jeffrey was full of anticipation. Leilani watched the people who boarded with them. For the third time since coming to the island, she noticed an unobtrusive Chinese who was dressed for business except that he casually kept his coat folded over his arm, hanging in front of his briefcase. Sentosa was small, and she had noticed several other people a number of times. But this one seemed out of place. As Leilani and Jeffrey disembarked at the museum, she noticed that the man stayed on the tram.

Jeffrey could think of nothing but the adventure ahead. He led the way into the old hospital, and they walked through the rooms one by one. All the rooms opened on a central veranda, and each room was filled with photographs of Singapore before, during, and after the Japanese invasion. The pictures were informative but not pleasant.

"I can see why they called it 'The Island of Leaving Death Behind,' " Leilani whispered to him. "There were an awful lot of deaths in this tiny place."

Finally, they came to the surrender chamber. The walls had been removed and replaced with glass. Inside, seated at two long tables, were twenty-seven life-size wax figures of the Japanese and British, a kitsch reenactment of the Japanese surrender in the style of "Early Tussaud," as Jeffrey whispered to Leilani. Jeffrey looked at the uniforms and the characters, concentrating on Lord Louis Mountbatten. Leilani watched the tourists.

"I was told there is a whole generation of people here who deeply resent even Japanese tourists," Jeffrey whispered to her.

"I can see why."

Then she saw him, standing well to the side and across from her, gazing directly at them: the Chinese man with the briefcase. He quickly looked away as she caught his gaze. She surreptitiously pointed him out to Jeffrey as they strolled down the path to the tram stop. The man followed well behind.

"What now?" Jeffrey asked. Leilani shrugged. The tram appeared almost immediately, and they boarded at the front. He got on toward the rear. Leilani and Jeffrey were silent, looking at the passing cultivated jungle. Finally, Leilani extracted the pamphlet from her purse and opened it on her lap. He inspected it with her.

"Let's take the cable car back," he whispered. "Might be time to ditch him before his car shows up." She nodded.

They hopped off the shuttle and walked into the imitation

Swiss chalet where the cableway lines were forming. They joined the queue. They were outside the boarding shed and could not see the cars themselves.

"I've got an idea. Walk up ahead of me and see how many people fit into each car." She looked at him, puzzled, then walked into the shed. She was back in a minute.

"Six. Only six, the sign says."

"Okay. See that family, with the three kids, right in front of our man?"

"Yes."

"Watch me play the child-loving American when it comes our turn to get on. You stick with me."

"What are you doing?"

"We'll never shake him. So I'm going to get him in the tram car with us and ask him what his business is."

"And then?"

"I'm working on it."

The line moved ahead by six more spaces.

"Better hurry," she said to him as they entered the shed and their turn to board drew near. The next car would be theirs. Just as it approached the platform, Jeffrey began his pantomime, an exaggerated show of standing back to count the people on line. He counted out loud, and people began to stare at him. Finally, he pulled Leilani with him several places down the line.

"Excuse me, sir," he said to a young Indian man who was standing with his wife and three children. "I was just counting. If we stand here you will be able to ride with your family. Otherwise, the count doesn't work out right." Jeffrey prayed he spoke English.

He never found out. The Indian's wife answered for him, thanking Jeffrey in perfect English. British English.

The Chinaman said nothing, even managed to hide his surprise. They moved through the turnstile and into their car. Jeffrey and Leilani sat down facing the Chinese man. An elderly couple sat beside him, a pretty young girl squeezed in beside

Leilani. Jeffrey watched the attendant standing beside the car release the gear and they bounced away.

Their cable car swung high out over Singapore harbor, and only the sound of the wind bouncing off its windows and the hum of the moving cable disturbed the absolute quiet. Below them, as far as they could see, were ships. Some appeared to be waiting, others had bumboats at their sides, piglets taking from giant sows. Those directly below the cableway were being unloaded in port, and machinery lined the docks everywhere: the economic miracle of Singapore in action. They had just bumped over the suspension tower rising out of the middle of the bay when Jeffrey looked directly at the Chinaman.

"What the hell are you after? Why are you following us?"

The man immediately covered his surprise and did not speak.

Leilani looked at him, too, as Jeffrey repeated his question. Finally he spoke.

"No speak English."

"You work for How or one of his gangster buddies, or are you a government gangster?"

The others in the car stared nervously at Jeffrey. He looked at the man with what he hoped was a withering glare.

"I think you understand English very well. Why are you following us?"

The man looked out the window, pretending to ignore them. As he did, he slid the coat from his arm and wedged it between his leg and the car wall. Only Leilani and Jeffrey could see him pull the butt of a black pistol out of his coat pocket and glare back at them. The threat was clear, and so was their great disadvantage.

The car began its slow descent toward the tower at the ferry building. When it was less than one hundred yards from the first stop, Jeffrey began rummaging around in his tote. Leilani looked at him as if he was out of his mind.

"The camera. I can't find the camera," he said.

"Camera?" He hadn't had one, she was sure of that. She

began searching her large purse, glancing at the pocket where she kept her gun and wishing it was there.

The car glided gracefully into the gap in the building, and its occupants—except for Jeffrey, who continued to rummage—began to shift, preparing anxiously to leave. The car swung to a stop and the attendant stepped away from the gear lever and opened the door.

Jeffrey could see people waiting to get on. He motioned Leilani out. "Go to the elevator. Hold a car," he whispered in her ear. Then he began an elaborate Alphonse-Gaston routine with the old couple and the young girl, insisting they crawl over him and exit first.

"Hurry, please," the attendant ordered.

"Yes, please hurry," Jeffrey repeated as he shifted about the car which was now bouncing on its mooring. "After you. Please. I insist." He kept the Chinaman behind him, blocking his passage.

"If you don't get out, the car will leave," the attendant insisted.

"Right. The car will leave." Jeffrey dropped his wet swimming suit, again blocking the Chinaman with his body. He looked up and could see the elevator door open across the landing. Leilani looked up at him as she moved to hold the door open.

In one very fast motion Jeffrey turned, scooped up his swimsuit, jumped from the car, slammed the door shut on the startled Chinese, pushed the stunned attendant aside, grabbed the gear lever, and released it. He heard the safety lock on the door snap shut as the car began to move.

The Chinaman began yelling—in English—ordering the attendant to stop the car, which bobbed out of the high rise and continued on its journey. The attendant, thoroughly confused, looked up in time to see Jeffrey run into the elevator as its doors closed.

"I'm impressed," Leilani said as they walked out of the building to a cab queue. "I wonder who he was."

"My guess is that he has nothing to do with the government.

Otherwise he'd have pulled out some ID, or actually shown his gun and made them stop the cableway. I think he's working for someone else. How probably."

"I wouldn't bet against it."

"I'm thirsty." Jeffrey was covered with sweat.

He was still complaining about being parched when they arrived back at the hotel half an hour later.

"Go take your shower. Then we'll meet in my room for drinks. My treat."

"I accept," he smiled.

He arrived to find that she had room-service hors d'oeuvres and a good supply of beer and liquor. That was what he noticed after he had seen Leilani herself: She was dressed in a sheer cotton muumuu. Her hair was pulled back and fell loosely to her shoulders, which were dark. She wore a delicate gold chain around her neck.

"Here," she said, handing him a beer. "This is where I teach you an old Hawaiian custom. We embrace to celebrate the end of an adventure, and then we drink to the future."

And so they did, except that another adventure of sorts was just beginning. He knew it the moment he felt her breasts, separated from him only by the cotton of her dress and the cotton of his shirt, touch his chest. Then her lips met his.

She kept her arm on his shoulder, her hand gently playing with the hair behind his ear. "What's your custom?"

"We *haoles* don't have many traditions. Instead, we embrace other cultures by imitating them."

They toasted again, and the third time Leilani kissed him there was no mistaking her intentions. He tried to resist her, but when she kissed him again, his resolve evaporated like a squall in a tropical wind.

She was incredibly sexual, seizing the initiative from him only to give it back for her pleasure. Afterward, as she played with the hair on his chest, she looked at him and smiled.

"You look like a man having a crisis of conscience. I'm sorry about that."

"So am I."

"It is our secret, and it will remain that. I promise."

"Me too," he said, and then, confused and feeling terribly guilty, he added, "And mine to live with."

"Now that I have seduced you, I will buy you dinner. At the International Bazaar, where we started."

"You're on." Then, with a weak smile, he kissed her gently.

They dressed, walked the short distance to the bazaar, and ate mostly in companionable silence. She asked him again about How, and this time he reported the entire encounter to her.

"That's it?" she said when he finished. He nodded. "Then I think your short version on the beach was the perfect condensation."

She wanted him to feel good, and so she took his hand as they walked back to the hotel. Along the way they passed several shims, some walking with their men.

"Do you suppose any of them imagine I'm your shim?"

They laughed and turned into the hotel's revolving doors. They found an entire reception committee waiting. Leilani spotted the American embassy official she had seen that morning, a man named Taylor. Then they both saw three uniformed policemen standing with C. D. Lee, who was dressed in his diplomatic pin-striped best.

"We're expected," Jeffrey muttered.

Taylor, looking harassed, took them aside immediately.

"They're going to return your passports. You've been cleared. And they're going to ask, for your own safety, that you leave the country immediately. In fact, they're going to insist on it. They're even going to drive you to the airport and see you onto a plane for Honolulu." He paused, removed a handkerchief from his pocket, and wiped the sweat from his forehead. "Just don't ask any questions."

"Do they know why she was here?" Jeffrey asked, nodding his head at Leilani.

"Absolutely. They permitted it, even gave her their blessing. But they'd never admit it. They're scared to death of the Chinese."

Leilani nodded. Jeffrey looked across at Lee, who was consulting with the two cops. He appeared to be holding a small package, but Jeffrey couldn't tell for sure, because Lee's back was toward him.

"Why is Lee here?" Leilani asked.

Taylor didn't miss a beat. "This is the Orient, Miss Martin. Things never are what they seem . . . especially with people like Lee. He's very closely connected—if not completely connected—to their secret service. Lee knows things. I'm certain he knows all about this business."

"Probably more than we do," Jeffrey added. "We were followed today. A Chinese . . . and he was armed. He wasn't working for the government."

"Maybe Lee has a point. He said he was concerned for your safety."

"He doesn't give a shit," Jeffrey said clearly, hoping Lee might hear him. "He's another bureaucrat . . . one with a computer chip on his shoulder."

"And a dangerous one," Leilani added.

Taylor nodded absently, then walked across to Lee and gestured in the direction of Jeffrey and Leilani. It was almost like a dance, this little ritual of polite diplomacy.

"Well then, this unpleasantness is over," Lee said, shaking each of their hands. "It is my pleasure to return your passports to you and also to apologize for any inconvenience. This entire business is most unfortunate."

"I'll say," Jeffrey muttered. Taylor and Leilani both shot him a look, willing him to keep quiet.

"These two policemen will help you pack your things and will escort you to the airport and onto the plane for Honolulu. You have time, if you wish, for a rest and for dinner. They will wait outside of your rooms."

"Thank you," Leilani said. She tried a smile, but when it didn't work she quickly gave up.

Then, almost as an afterthought, Lee handed a package to Jeffrey. "This, I believe, belongs to you, Mr. Dean."

Jeffrey took it, nodding, afraid that if he spoke he would lose his temper again.

"The whole thing is bullshit," he muttered as he and Leilani stepped into the elevator, the two cops right beside them. He quickly ripped the package open, certain of its contents. He was right: There, polished brightly, was his missing shoe.

"I wish they'd send someone to polish the other one," he muttered. Leilani smiled at him.

Lee, thorough to the last detail, had arranged for Leilani to fly first class along with Jeffrey. They were buckled into their seats, and the plane was on the runway ready to take off on the long transpacific flight.

"I've still got Lee's Agatha Christie. And the bill for it."

"What?" She knew nothing about it.

"Nothing important." The book would be easy enough to sell back in Los Angeles.

"You still stopping in Honolulu for a couple of days?" Leilani asked him. The question was rhetorical, but she was uncomfortable and trying to make conversation.

"Yes. Rachel is meeting me. We're going to have a holiday of sorts."

The inevitable awkwardness slowed them both. A shared experience was ending, one that had turned intimate only hours before. Jeffrey was not the sort of man to leave his conscience on the rumpled sheets of his passion. Leilani, on the other hand, was far less troubled by it. She had other things on her mind than the pleasant memory of his body.

"Then you'll be there when the *Marara* docks at Pearl Harbor?"

"Yes and no. I will be in Honolulu. I won't be at Pearl Harbor."

"Then you're the lucky one," she said. The big Singapore Airlines 747 started its long run for takeoff.

15

By the clock, because of the International Dateline, Jeffrey and Leilani arrived in Honolulu before they left Singapore. They arrived blurry-eyed, dehydrated, and tired. Their farewell to one another was not quite a handshake and not quite romantic either. She wished him luck. He said she'd need it more than he did. She nodded and smiled, and then they separated, gratefully. She was, she said, going to her apartment to sleep a while. He headed for the rank of car rental lines, then to the Kahala Hilton to sleep and wait for Rachel.

Eddie Alvaraz, already in Honolulu and feeling cheerful after his rendezvous with Diane, paid a call on the Honolulu Police Department. He introduced himself in his capacity as an investigator for the International Foundation for Art Research, and added that he was also an LAPD detective. The latter, rather than the former, established his bona fides—and got him the cooperation of the Honolulu police. It also brought him permission to use the department's computer.

He didn't find much. Alfred Davidson merited only a brief mention—four years previously, the police had responded to a call from his Kahala Avenue home. Davidson himself had called for protection from the angry about-to-be-ex–Mrs. Davidson.

Not a success story with women, Eddie noted. Nor much of a success at business just now. He wrote down Davidson's unlisted home address and telephone number from the file, then headed off to the offices of the *Honolulu Bulletin*.

Its library turned up only one item he hadn't already seen. An article in the financial pages two days ago announced the year-end bad news for TransPac and Davidson. Income down forty percent, with a large loss posted. There was, as is usual in such instances, a brief quote from Davidson at the end of the story expressing great optimism for the company's future and calling the current setbacks "strictly cyclical, clearly temporary"—and one of those shibboleths of big business, "a market adjustment." Eddie shook his head in wonder at the ritual of businessmen dealing with bad news: they almost always found something hopeful to say, even if they were lying. He was certain Davidson was lying.

From the *Bulletin*'s offices he drove the short distance to the Federal Building and found his way to the Treasury Department's Customs office. There he met Mark O'Brien, the head of the bureau. O'Brien appeared distracted and busy, but was polite nevertheless. When he walked Eddie into the room full of agents' desks, Eddie could see a busy bureau at work. There was little of the federal bureaucratic laziness apparent—every agent seemed to be occupied, and phones were ringing constantly.

"Mostly investigations and inquiries from here," O'Brien explained. "The real work we do mostly at the airport and at the docks." O'Brien paused by an unoccupied desk and rapped his knuckles on it.

"Leilani isn't here," he explained to Eddie. "But she should be. She said she'd be in."

Eddie couldn't decide if O'Brien was frustrated because Leilani wasn't there or because he might have Eddie on his hands longer than he had anticipated.

"It's okay, I can wait."

He didn't wait long. Within five minutes, Carl Spelling appeared in the doorway, stopped to talk to one of the agents, and then approached Eddie.

"Leilani called. She's running late and will meet us at the restaurant."

"We presumed you'd want to eat lunch," the Chinese who had materialized behind him said. "I'm Roger Chow . . . the third member of this triumvirate." His smile was broad and genuine.

They shook hands. Eddie instinctively liked Chow, sensed the unspoken understanding that they were both outsiders in the culture they lived in. Chow escorted them to a Chinese restaurant less than two blocks from the Federal Building where he was clearly a favored customer.

"These Chinese are thick as thieves . . . all of them," Spelling joked as they sat down.

"The food will be better," Eddie said.

Chow plainly liked the comment, and immediately began chattering in Chinese to the waiter. Appetizers appeared almost immediately.

"I was right. Delicious," Eddie said between mouthfuls. "Now about Davidson."

"We've got nothing on him . . . absolutely nothing," Spelling said. "And we've checked everything."

Chow interrupted. "What I've got is a strong intuition."

"Me too," Eddie said.

"Then how's he bringing it in?" Spelling stopped eating to wait for an answer.

Eddie had one, or thought he had, but he decided to wait and see what was presented to him first. He wasn't about to share information on a one-way track. The silence of the impasse was brief. Chow ended it by waving to a woman at the front of the restaurant.

Leilani was, Eddie realized with a start, beautiful. Not at all what he'd expected in a native Hawaiian customs agent. Not even what he'd come to expect from a female agent of any race. He could barely hide his surprise, and he sensed that she knew all too well the impact she had on people.

"I'm curious to know what happened in Singapore. Maybe

we can all compare notes and see what breaks loose," Eddie said.

Leilani stuck directly to the facts, and nothing extra. She explained that in Singapore she had picked up a trail of the jade from a shim who was subsequently murdered.

"She was selling information and I was buying. What I got from her was a shipping report from the *Singapore Times*. She had circled a ship called the *Marara*."

Eddie explained how he, too, had come up with the ship's name, and his encounter with the Korean who had worked for Herman Roh.

"Roh has people over here," Roger Chow chimed in. "I've seen the name on our computer."

"How do we get to the *Marara?*"

"That's all arranged," Spelling said, leaning back in his chair and looking expansive. The meal, really a small feast, had arrived, and all of their plates were full. Between mouthfuls, Spelling and Chow explained what they'd arranged.

"When the *Marara* docks at Pearl tomorrow morning, we'll be there."

"In force," Chow added. "We're going to go through that ship and find the jade. I've even brought out three crews from the airport so there will be a whole platoon of agents to go through the ship."

"May I come along?"

Eddie saw the reactions of Leilani and Spelling, and knew they didn't want him present. Chow seemed to agree with them, yet when he spoke it was not what Eddie expected.

"As a spectator, yes. But regulations forbid you from participating."

Eddie nodded. He understood, even if he didn't much like it—and he particularly understood regulations. It seemed to him at times that the LAPD was absolutely paralyzed by them.

Giving him her best smile, Leilani adroitly changed the subject. "I understand you've done graduate work in art history."

"Yes."

"Me too," she smiled.

Eddie realized that his look of surprise must have been obvious, but any embarrassment quickly vanished as they compared notes about Stanford versus USC, the perils of thesis advisers, and how their education had changed their careers. She seemed particularly intrigued by IFAR, and because she knew only a little about it she had many questions.

Eddie agreed to meet them late the following morning at the Federal Building and to accompany them to the *Marara*. He was optimistic that something would turn up. He was convinced that Davidson was the man behind the smuggling, but he was worried about the lack of evidence—or even of a secure lead.

After lunch, he drove to the outskirts of the city and onto Kahala, winding along between the mountainside and the splendid seafront homes. When he came to the house he was looking for, he passed and parked. Alfred Davidson lived in one of the most impressive of an already impressive row of homes. Even his driveway had a view of the waterfront. The house itself was contemporary, with two wings off either side of the main structure, and a double front door made of teak. There were four cars in the garage, a Ford station wagon, a Toyota van, a Mercedes 450 SL convertible, and a brand new BMW sedan.

There was no sign of life, just all of the indications of people who lived very well indeed. Eddie strolled several houses away in either direction, returning each time to Davidson's. In half an hour, when he had seen nobody and knew his strolling wouldn't seem nonchalant much longer to anyone who might be watching, he left.

He had no more sense of Davidson than what he had brought with him from Los Angeles, and he was uncertain what to do next. He got his answer when he arrived back at the Holiday Inn. There was a message from Leilani, and he called her immediately.

"There's an art show and a charity auction of jade at Pacific Gallery tonight," she told him. "I just found out about it. Davidson probably will be there. Carl is going. So am I."

"No invitation needed?" he asked, reaching for his notepad.

"Not a thing."

"I have the address, and thanks. I'll be there." He checked off Davidson's gallery from his list of visits to be made. Good timing, he thought to himself; it turns out to be an annual event. Eddie had an obsession about being well organized. He would have been there anyway, once he had found out about it, but now he could spend the day applying other checks to his list.

Eddie kicked off his shoes and lay down on the bed. He was just dozing off when the telephone rang again.

"I called in sick with an earache," Diane told him. "I'm staying overnight. Are you available?"

"Earache?" Eddie thought it a pretty poor excuse for not working, certainly one that would be greeted with skepticism.

"Earache. If you fly, it works every time. Well?"

He suggested they meet immediately for a drink, then have dinner later. She accepted.

"How about your room instead?" He surprised himself when he said it. In the throes of a crush, Eddie could startle even himself.

"We'll order something from room service," she agreed. "Room 314. See you in a couple of minutes."

His grin was sheepish as she opened the door, and she smiled shyly. They kissed briefly and he tucked a stray strand of her hair back in place. She was once again in jeans, sandals, and a brightly colored blouse.

"Coffee . . . tea . . . or me?" she said, reaching for the phone.

"Whichever's easier to make," he replied.

"Oh my God. I actually said that." Her face was bright red.

"So did I," he laughed. "So did I."

16

To his way of thinking, it was the perfect method for dealing with jet lag: swim and sleep. He left his hotel room and headed for the Kahala's private beach.

He didn't quite make it to the water on the first try. The attendant issued him a big beach towel, which he placed in the shade. He lay down and almost immediately fell asleep. It was over an hour later when he awoke, glanced up at a surant palm, and felt the sweat beading on his chest. He walked into the water, submerged himself, swam out to the diving platform and back. It was a ritual, a slow dance of narcissism, performed by millions before him. After two more short naps broken by two cooling swims, he was refreshed and ready to go.

The room had a magnificent view of Diamond Head, Koko Head, and the dolphin pool that separated the hotel from the beach. He showered, wrapped himself in a towel, and ate a room service lunch on his balcony. Then he consulted the yellow pages, made a short list, and drove to Honolulu.

Both used bookshops were on King Street. It was not necessarily a good part of town, but the area was cleaned by the trade winds and consequently better-looking than similar neighborhoods in the States. Even the porno shops had to try hard to look seedy. In the first bookstore, he found nothing of interest. In the second, just a few doors away, on a dusty bottom shelf at the back of the store, his roving eye nearly skipped over a book, but he caught himself and reached for it.

It was among a group of books on sailing, and he nearly missed it because of the way it was wedged into a corner. His heart raced and he felt light-headed the moment he saw it. That alone was enough to tell him he'd found something. And he had: *Mutiny on the Bounty.* He opened it carefully—the pages were beginning to separate from the binding—and beheld the inscription: "To Dr. John M. Trask, with best wishes from James Norman Hall, Tahiti, February 10th 1933." Beneath the inscription was the signature of "Chas Nordhoff." A small glossy black-and-white photo of Hall had been pasted at the bottom of the page. Holding his breath, he turned to the copyright page: October 1932—a first edition.

He quickly scanned the shelves to be certain the other two novels of the *Bounty* trilogy weren't there. They weren't. The three novels were seldom, if ever, found together except in a very few collections. Inscribed copies were even rarer. He leaned against the bookcase and inspected the book. He loved its musty smell. He had loved that smell since he was a boy. The book was in very good condition for a volume so old. Even the dust jacket had somehow miraculously survived the years with a minimum of tears. He looked at the cover with its drawing of Captain Bligh and his men departing in their longboat, the mutineers of the *Bounty* lined up on the ship's aft deck waving them away.

It was a small treasure, one of those wonderful moments book dealers live for. The only hurdle would be the shopkeeper. Did he know what he had? Jeffrey's guess, because there was no price marked in the book and no effort at all made to display it, was that no one here was aware of it.

The Japanese shopkeeper looked up and smiled as Jeffrey asked how much the book cost.

"Which shelf?" the man asked.

"What?"

"Which shelf was it on?"

"That one back there." Jeffrey pointed at the shelf at the back of the shop.

"Those are all three dollars each."

The friendly Japanese not only didn't inspect the book, he didn't even look at it. Jeffrey kept it grasped in his wet palm the whole time, even as he fished in his other hand for the money in his pocket.

He didn't even risk asking for a bag. Instead, he left the store immediately and went to his car, where he sat for several minutes examining the book. He was elated, in part because of the lucky find, but also because he could resell it easily for at least a thousand dollars.

An hour later, when Rachel walked off her plane, Jeffrey was waiting with a big grin and an even bigger lei made of fragrant frangipani blossoms. He had bought one for her and was wearing one himself.

"You don't look like a man who's been disappointed in Singapore," she smiled at him, giving him a gentle kiss and a knowing look.

"I'm not . . . not anymore." He told her about the book in what she recognized as his happiest, most enthusiastic voice.

She gasped in pleasure as he showed her into their room at the Kahala. "I think one of the reasons I love you is because you stay in first-class hotels," she said as she stepped out of her dress and began unpacking.

They talked—"housekeeping talk," as she always called it. The first subject was a report on his teenage son. Michael now had a car, a bright red Mitsubishi Turbo, and, like most boys with their first car, he was taking advantage of his sudden freedom. Jeffrey laughed as she described his constant coming and going, his new habit of doing his homework in the car, and a girl he had met and started dating—tentatively but with great ardor.

"That at least explains why he hasn't been there. I've called him three times since I got here this morning."

Rachel took a long bath, and Jeffrey once again fell briefly asleep. He awoke to find her, wrapped in a towel, her long dark hair pinned up, sitting beside him on the bed. He reached up and pulled the pins out of her hair, watching it fall across her back. Then he tugged at her towel.

"You first," she smiled at him. "I want to see how much you want me."

"I'll give you a hint. Here." He took her hand.

In a great rush, his guilt consumed him. He tried rationalizing his behavior with Leilani first: It made sex with Rachel better; he had been seduced; and on and on. Nothing worked. He wanted to beg her forgiveness . . . but he couldn't unless he told her, and right now that was impossible.

"That should do just fine," she said, bending down to kiss him as her towel fell away.

They had been lovers for seven years, as passionately committed to one another as they were to their respective independence. There was little eagerness about them now, and much more certainty. Where others fell into routine, they fell into a variable ritual of what pleased them most, yet there was nothing perfunctory about it.

Afterward, he kissed the light sheen of sweat between her breasts, and silently cursed the hoary old belief that sex away from home base made the home front more exciting. Cursed it because it seemed to be true.

"How do I shape up against the women in Singapore?" She was teasing him, yet he was also aware that between them there had never been a commitment of monogamy. Or perhaps there had been, but unspoken.

"The interesting thing is, they aren't all girls," he said. Then he told her, to her great amusement, about the shims. And he told her much else that had happened, with one significant omission.

Rachel was a very good listener, and her dark, watchful eyes hardly left his face as he explained all that had gone wrong in Singapore. "The customs agent . . . what happened to her?"

"She came back with me. They kicked her out at the same time."

"You should be proud of yourself," she smiled, touching a finger to his lips.

"Why?"

"It must take some doing to be declared persona non grata in a place like that."

"In my case it was easy. All I had to do was show up."

He got out of bed, went to the dressing area, where he opened the hotel's well-stocked refrigerator and began snacking on the expensive little bags of Macadamia nuts, cheese, and fresh pineapple. Rachel grinned. With Jeffrey, she could always tell how good the sex was by how much he ate afterward.

They dressed, and while Rachel looked over the various brochures the hotel placed in their room, Jeffrey examined *Mutiny on the Bounty* again, shaking his head with pleasure at the memory of finding it.

"Ah!" Rachel said, pushing her reading glasses back up her nose. "Here's something I want to do. Six to eight. A gallery show of local contemporary art, plus—this should interest you—some of the owner's rare jade collection. A place called Pacific Gallery."

"You've got a date."

"Actually, I don't recall asking you."

"Then try and get rid of me."

17

Pacific Gallery was on Merchant Street in the financial district, a location suitable for both the gallery's pretense and its clientele. Its name and business hours were printed in neat black letters on the door. In the window were two big paintings, abstracts striking for their concordant mixture of sun-bleached colors contrasting with a forceful and verdant green. They demanded attention, and they got it as guests arrived for the opening.

There was a dense crowd of people in the downstairs gallery, which Rachel, a gallery-owner herself, interpreted as good for business. She was struck by the character of the Honolulu gallery crowd. In Los Angeles, despite the relatively benign climate, people dressed up more; here they were studiously and elegantly casual. There was hardly a tie or a pair of high heels in the crowd.

A waiter passed with a tray of plastic glasses filled with white wine. Jeffrey took one for himself and another for Rachel. They began to circulate and examine the art, unlike many in the room who seemed more intent on the people. It wasn't until they squeezed their way upstairs that they found the jade. The upstairs gallery was smaller, with long, narrow glass cases standing on carved wooden legs. Along one wall—Jeffrey assumed it was reserved for the most valuable pieces—were a series of small windows, each containing two or three pieces of perfectly lighted jade. Perfectly protected, too, he thought.

The first piece they saw was one of the best, certainly the most remarkable. It was an exquisitely detailed carving of a cabbage, made of jadeite, its stalk pristine white, the leaves a smooth green with a mix of white and green veins. It rested, ideally poised, on a teak stand. In the lower right-hand corner of the window was a small sign identifying it as from the Ch'ing dynasty, 1644–1912.

They stared at it, overcome by its gentle beauty, struck by its relative youth compared to most of the jade in the room. Next to it, in an adjoining window, was a jade winged beast, identified as Pi Hsieh.

"Han dynasty, 206 B.C. to 220 A.D.," Rachel read aloud.

It was some time before they turned away from the jade and began to observe the other guests. In this, the upstairs gallery, the visitors were primarily Chinese and Japanese.

"You have to wonder if it is some kind of genetic imprint," Jeffrey mused, almost to himself.

"What do you mean?" Rachel sipped her wine.

"What jade means, its incredible significance. I doubt if anyone but an Asian can understand it. It goes back generations and generations. I wonder if the man who owns all of this really understands it."

"Probably understands its value. I promise you that." Jeffrey nodded and looked across the room to see a tall, patrician-looking man surrounded by others, all of whom seemed to be paying rapt attention to his words. Alone among the people in this room he was wearing a tropical suit, clearly tailor-made, and a silk necktie.

Rachel had turned again to the jade, but Jeffrey watched the man, and then began to inspect the people around him. Two of them had their backs to him, but when one of them—a woman—turned, Jeffrey muttered, loud enough for Rachel to hear, "Well, what do you know."

"What?" Rachel asked, hardly shifting her gaze from the jade.

"That woman, standing next to the well-dressed man," Jeffrey said, moving toward the small group. "Leilani!" He was genuinely surprised to see her, but not as surprised as she was when she heard her name, turned, and saw him approach.

She quickly stepped away from the group surrounding the man, but hardly far enough.

"What are you doing here?" she hissed at him.

Jeffrey was only slightly taken aback. He was now accustomed to Leilani's sudden appearances and disappearances. "Rachel, this is Leilani Martin . . . we met in Singapore. Leilani, this is Rachel Sabin."

"My name only. Don't say what I do," Leilani whispered to them. Then, self-consciously, she reached out and shook hands with Rachel. Rachel was instinctively wary of this remarkable-looking Hawaiian woman. She extended her hand, and smiled in her most noncommittal manner.

If encountering Jeffrey surprised Leilani, it was nothing compared to what happened next. Rachel looked away from her and toward the gathering immediately behind. This time, the smile of recognition spread across her face. Jeffrey heard someone behind him say, "Rachel . . . Rachel," looked up, and there was Eddie Alvaraz, stepping away from the ever-shrinking group.

Eddie hugged Rachel and grinned as she gave him a kiss on the cheek. Then he stuck out his hand toward Jeffrey, and instead of shaking it, he grasped the extended hand and pulled Jeffrey toward him and hugged him too.

"Old friends," Eddie explained to Leilani. Then he began to introduce her. Both Leilani and Jeffrey spoke at the same time.

"We've already met," Jeffrey explained. It occurred to him that Leilani and Eddie weren't at the gallery for their pleasure or enlightenment. "This is business, I take it?" he asked politely.

Eddie's eyes flashed at him and he nodded. Both Jeffrey and

Rachel knew Eddie as a friend. But they were well aware of his work, and considered him an astute judge of art.

"We're at the Kahala Hilton, Eddie. Give us a call, will you—we're just leaving." He wanted out. Quick. But his attempt to extricate himself and Rachel was too late.

"I'm Alfred Davidson," the tall, patrician man said. "And this is Carl . . . I'm sorry, I've forgotten your last name."

"Spelling." He too was tall, a patrician in the making, but for now just blond and too good-looking.

"Mr. Spelling is a friend of mine," Leilani said, thinking fast, trying to find a way out. "We were here to look at this wonderful jade."

"Remarkable, isn't it?" Rachel added.

"Thank you," Davidson said.

"It was Leilani I was telling you about." Jeffrey was now thoroughly disoriented, and the words were hardly out of his mouth when he realized his tactical error.

"Yes. We met through the art department at the university," Leilani lied easily.

Now they all understood, if not what was going on, at least what the rules of the encounter were to be. No further explanation was necessary, because Rachel had asked Davidson about a particular piece of jade, a vase dating back to the Ming Dynasty. Davidson, seemingly eager to talk about it, began a discourse. Eddie, Leilani, Jeffrey, and the man named Spelling were left standing together.

"We're here on business," Leilani whispered to him. "The jade. So be careful. Please."

"It's all right, Leilani," Jeffrey smiled easily. "I was just going to excuse myself and go to the men's room." He could see Davidson and Rachel turning back to them.

"It's that way," Spelling said, pointing toward a teak-paneled door at the rear of the room.

Jeffrey walked through the doorway into a carpeted small hallway where he found two identical doors. Before he could wonder which might be the bathroom, he tried the door on his right. It was locked and a female voice called out "Occupied. Through in a minute." Jeffrey turned and tried the other door, hoping it might be another bathroom.

It wasn't. The door opened to reveal a small, elegantly appointed office. To his right, on the wall facing into the gallery, was a one-way mirror. He could see Rachel and Leilani talking with Eddie, so he paused a moment to relish the harmless voyeurism. Davidson and the other man, Spelling, had moved off in opposite directions. He noticed Davidson nod at Spelling, then signal him in the direction of Leilani, Rachel, and Eddie. Spelling acknowledged the gesture and walked back toward the conversation he had just left.

To his left, across the office and immediately to the right of the large desk, was another door. The light was on, and Jeffrey could see that it too was a bathroom. He stepped inside and closed the door. When he emerged a moment later, he shut off the light, plunging the whole office into darkness. Before he could turn around and find the light switch again, he collided with the desk and tipped over the wastebasket beside it.

He turned on the light and quickly bent down to pick up the contents of the basket. He stuffed a fistful of papers back in, and gingerly began to pick up the cigarette butts he had spilled. There were too many, so he extracted a small piece of cardboard which hadn't fallen out and began to scrape them off the carpet, cursing to himself.

He dropped the cigarettes into the wastebasket, and was about to toss in the cardboard, when he noticed that it seemed oddly heavy. He turned it over, holding it up to the light falling from the bathroom.

The other side was bright blue and had a small piece of marble glued to the center of it. It was, the bold printing at the top of the cardboard said, "A Genuine Piece of the *Arizona* Memorial." There was a gaudy exclamation mark after the headline. A tourist souvenir. On it, written in neat red ink, was the number 2400. He looked at it for a few seconds, tossed it back into the wastebasket, and returned to the gallery. It reminded him that he wanted to visit the *Arizona* Memorial in Pearl Harbor.

He found Rachel downstairs, looking at the paintings, appraising them with her professional eye.

"Good?"

"Interesting, but not good enough."

"Where did the others go?"

"They split up as quickly as they could. Is something going on?"

"Apparently. Probably has to do with the jade smuggling."

"Is this Davidson man involved?"

"Possibly, but who knows?"

She nodded, clearly distracted. She put her glass down, refused another from the waiter who rushed to pick up her empty, and turned to Jeffrey.

"Shall we go?" On their way out they saw Leilani, Eddie, and Carl Spelling standing together near the center of the room. Eddie saw them and quickly walked up.

"Breakfast tomorrow. Your hotel?" The first was a statement, the second a question. They understood immediately.

"Ten o'clock all right?"

"Late . . . but okay."

"We're on vacation, Eddie. Not business," Rachel reminded him.

Rachel was silent as they drove back to the hotel. As they turned onto Kahala Avenue, she spoke: "You didn't tell me sweet Leilani was such a heavenly flower."

"Hmm. Didn't seem important." Jeffrey's complicated guilt mechanism began to grind. Yet he could not help but find pleasure in Rachel's jealousy.

"Did you?"

"I gave it a thought or two."

She looked directly into his eyes: "Jeffrey, I can understand your wanting her. After all, you're human. And I suppose I should be philosophical about it like the mature worldly woman

I'm supposed to be. But I *would* cry, and I suppose that more than anything else would infuriate me."

"I see."

"No, my dear, you don't."

She put her arm up on the back of the seat, and moved her hand toward his ear. She caressed him. Whether it was pleasure at her touch or relief the crisis had passed—a crisis which had started so many months before for them both—she couldn't tell, but he breathed deeply, turned to her, and smiled.

18

They ate a room-service breakfast, relishing the view of the white beach between Diamond Head and Koko Head, the azure blue water, the waves breaking over the distant coral reef. Jeffrey and Eddie ate heartily; Rachel, no great morning eater, picked at her food. While they ate, the conversation was strictly social. Encouraged by Eddie, Rachel talked about the remodeling of her gallery, its increasing size and success. Jeffrey, who had heard it all, and often, tried very hard to look interested.

"At least it gives you time off to go away together," Eddie said at last. "Who's minding your store, Jeffrey?"

They both answered at once: Rachel was. It was a task that required little of her time—it was the slow season in the rare-book business: too soon after Christmas to sell, and too soon to collect on his larger preholiday sales.

"I return telephone calls and take the checks to the bank," she explained.

"What checks there are," Jeffrey added.

"Eddie, Jeffrey was growing a bit tired of the book business and started missing the action." Then, with a cryptic glance at Jeffrey, she continued. "At least that's what he says. Anyhow, that's how he ended up in Singapore, writing a book."

"Or not writing a book." Jeffrey put his bare feet up on the wrought-iron railing and put his arms behind his head. Then he told his version—Eddie had already heard Leilani's—of what happened in Singapore.

"Your turn," Jeffrey said to Eddie when he'd finished.

Eddie told them about TransPac, Alfred Davidson, the reason he and Leilani had been at Pacific Gallery the previous night, and his suspicion that Davidson was somehow involved.

"You can't make a lot of progress on instinct, but I swear I know a psychopath when I see one. The money and position only provide camouflage. No evidence, that's the problem. I need the jade for evidence. The *Marara* pulls into Pearl in about an hour. Leilani and I will be there, along with her customs cohort, the guy named Spelling you met last night."

"He's a customs agent?" Jeffrey seemed surprised.

"Why are you surprised?"

"I somehow thought he was with Davidson. Obviously, I was wrong."

"And obviously I better get going," Eddie said, delivering Jeffrey a pat on the back and Rachel a kiss on the cheek. "Duty awaits."

Rachel could hardly wait for the door to close.

"I've got an idea. Why don't I call the Pacific Gallery and—under some pretext or another—see if I can get an appointment to look at the jade. We'll be buyers . . . big buyers. Let's go shopping."

"He'll recognize us from last night."

"So what? No problem there—it just confirms our interest."

Jeffrey paused, wondering briefly how to state his reservations. "I told them I was out of it."

"Aren't you curious?"

It was easy. Rachel, no stranger to playing a gallery owner, made the appointment for late that afternoon.

"Perfect," Jeffrey said to her when she hung up. "First, a short run for me, then we're off on a tour of Pearl Harbor. I want to see how it is the Japanese won the war after it was over."

"I don't think you'll find the answer there," Rachel laughed.

It was perfect weather for a run, a cool breeze, sunlight streaming through gigantic cumulus clouds. By his estimation he had run a mile and a half down Kahala toward Honolulu, when he turned and headed back toward the hotel. He was high on endorphins and his consciousness was far from Honolulu when he jogged right to pass a car parked along the shoulder.

"Mr. Dean . . . Mr. Dean, a moment please!"

Jeffrey froze. The familiar voice brought him rocketing back to reality. A reality he'd have preferred never to encounter again.

"Thank you. I was afraid I'd have to run to catch up to you and I dislike exercise." It was How, outfitted in a Hawaiian shirt, Bermudas, and sandals—under which were bright-colored argyle socks.

"How, you don't look like an ordinary tourist. You look like the tourist from hell." Jeffrey realized he felt safer because he was on American soil. The knowledge diminished his fear, but didn't erase it.

"Ah, but that's what I am."

"What the hell are you talking about?"

"In time, Mr. Dean. In time. I've acquired some information since I saw you last."

"Did someone die for it?"

"Not when I was there . . . but perhaps afterward. Who knows?"

How let Jeffrey absorb the implied threat before he continued.

"I think I know how it's going to happen, Mr. Dean, but I don't know when. I intend to find out. Soon, very soon . . . or it will be too late."

"For you."

"For a lot of people, yourself included. Does your lovely lady know about you and Miss Martin in Singapore?"

"None of your goddamn business."

"Your friend from IFAR . . . the Mexican gentleman. What has he told you?"

"Very little. We're social friends and we don't do business together."

"What is 'very little.' Be quick."

Jeffrey decided to hell with it—How probably knew anyway. "A man named Alfred Davidson. They suspect he is smuggling the jade into this country."

"And who is taking it out of China?"

"I haven't any idea. You can find that out for yourself."

How smiled, then turned back toward his car.

"I'll see you later. Perhaps then you will know more."

"I doubt it very much," Jeffrey said, resuming his run. "Fuck off, How . . . gangsters don't have it so easy here. We don't intimidate. You do understand the word intimidate, don't you?"

How turned from his car, the anger showing on his face. "Of course, Mr. Dean. I was educated at UCLA. I can even speak the initials without sounding like a parody of a Chinese."

"UCLA. Interesting. University of Caucasians Lost Among Asians, I take it you mean."

"And tomorrow the world, Mr. Dean. That is the business that interests me the most."

Jeffrey and Rachel arrived at Pearl Harbor at the same time as two busloads of Japanese tourists.

"No answers, but a lot of clues," he whispered to Rachel as they were shown into the theater where the tour began, feeling for all the world like two Occidentals in a veritable sea of Asians. Jeffrey spotted a handful of others Westerners, but not many, by the time the lights dimmed and the movie began. It lasted twenty minutes and presented the tourists with a dramatic and meticulously varnished account of the day of infamy in 1941.

"What do you mean, varnished?" Rachel asked as they walked out of the theater and onto the boarding area

"There's more to it than just that. I mean, didn't Roosevelt know? There has been argument about that for years. I think he had been warned. A lot of what was said in there is propaganda ... . not a lie, but not the whole truth."

"Today you are guests of the United States Navy," the uniformed guide declared as the small boat, crammed with tourists, set off on the short shuttle across the bay. "From here you can see that there are twenty-one windows on the *Arizona* Memorial—seven on each side and seven on top. They represent a perpetual twenty-one-gun salute to the 1,102 men who are still on board the ship."

Rachel shuddered. Jeffrey reached across and pulled out the camera from Rachel's tote bag. Neither of them was prepared for the impact of stepping onto the memorial itself. The first thing Jeffrey saw as they stepped through the entrance and onto the large, narrow open area was the body of the ship itself, a great rusting wreck still leaking oil, still holding the bodies of the men who died early that Sunday morning in 1941. Great, majestic clouds floated in the impossibly blue sky and the trade wind blew, as if to soothe the impact of all the death upon which they stood.

Rachel made no attempt to hide her tears. When the public address system began to play its recording of the sounds of that day, she saw the columns of names inscribed on the back wall of the memorial. Within a few seconds she had found two sets of brothers.

"I can't believe this," Jeffrey said, as she fished for a tissue. "I had no idea it was like this."

"It's the most popular tourist attraction in the Pacific," a guard standing by them said. "Would you like me to take your picture?"

He posed Jeffrey and Rachel with their backs to what was once the battleship's mighty gun turrets, now great gaping holes barely above the water line. Then, like everyone else, Rachel peered over the edge and into the dead battleship below. Jeffrey turned to the guard.

"Are there always so many Japanese tourists?" he asked quietly.

The guard was Hawaiian and wore a National Parks uniform. He smiled.

"Weird, isn't it? They almost all bow as they come on the memorial itself, I guess out of respect for the dead. Took me a year after they started coming in big numbers to figure out what was happening."

"And that is?"

"You a reporter or something? We're really not supposed to talk about it."

"No, just a tourist. A curious tourist."

"Almost all these people just got off a 747 nonstop from Tokyo. The tourist agencies over there block-book them onto the planes for a Hawaiian holiday. So many of them are coming here now, it's impossible for the tour groups to know how many are going to show up until they get off the plane. They might be exhausted and jet-lagged, but the agencies put them on buses and bring them right here. The tour leader counts heads on the bus and while the customers tour Pearl Harbor, they go to the pay phones just outside the gate and block-book the hotel rooms. It's a whole industry."

"And history just happened to make all this a convenient part of it."

The guard nodded and moved off to take some more pictures. Jeffrey returned to Rachel, and together they looked out across the bay. There, he saw it, at the great concrete pier directly across from them, its name clearly written on its bow.

"Look. There it is. The *Marara*. Unloading." Several trucks were parked at the pier, and two straining cranes were pulling the cargo out of the holds.

"Must be like looking for a needle in a haystack," Rachel said, shielding her eyes from the afternoon sun. "But that's what customs agents are trained to do. Do you think there is jade on board?"

"Yeah. We're all sure there is. What nobody can figure out

is how they're getting it off." Jeffrey looked down into the *Arizona* one last time as they boarded the boat for the other side of the harbor. "God, it's eerie. Imagine what it's like down there."

Rachel shuddered once again. "Time to go visit the Pacific Gallery."

19

They were shown into Alfred Davidson's office by an elegant, serene Chinese woman who was both polite to guests and deferential to her powerful employer. Rachel could see that Jeffrey was impressed. She herself thought the whole thing a sham, strictly appearances for appearances' sake.

Appearances obviously mattered a great deal to Davidson. Once again he wore a necktie. His tailored coat was perfectly in place, along with his manners. He did not acknowledge them from the gallery reception, yet both Jeffrey and Rachel were certain he remembered them.

"I understand you are looking for some old and good jade. How can I help?"

"Are any of the pieces from your current show on sale?" Jeffrey asked.

"Two were . . . or rather were part of a silent auction to raise money for the Honolulu Artists Program. Those have been sold. The others, I regret to say, are part of my private collection."

"But you do have pieces for sale?" Jeffrey suddenly wondered if they had misunderstood.

"Perhaps. It depends on many things. For instance, I should like to know who your customer is. Please don't think I'm asking inappropriate questions, but with jade such things matter. I am a well-known collector. I am also an Occidental man living in a racially mixed society, especially here in Honolulu. I mean to show the greatest respect."

Rachel believed him. Almost. "Our client . . . for now . . . prefers to remain anonymous. He is American, from the Midwest, and a very successful shopping center developer."

Davidson looked slightly skeptical, and formed a steeple with his long manicured fingers.

"With a Japanese wife." Jeffrey's contribution hadn't been rehearsed—it was an on-the-spot inspiration. It worked.

"Then I think I can understand why he is interested in jade. It was first his wife's great interest, am I correct?"

"Yes." Rachel wanted to turn and congratulate Jeffrey. Instead, she nodded at Davidson as if he, too, was a conspirator in art salesmanship.

"And what might they be interested in?" If Davidson was feeding chum to curious sharks, he wasn't letting on.

Now came the hard part. She had thought carefully and based her decision on what Eddie had told her about the jade already discovered, about Leilani's conversations as reported by Jeffrey, and on some hasty research she had done on the telephone with a helpful curator at the University of Hawaii. She opened her purse and consulted her list.

She read off several dynasties—from before and after the birth of Christ. She discussed her clients' interest in ritual pieces, burial pieces, and, all in all, tried to make their fascination with objects Oriental sound as catholic as possible.

Davidson merely nodded, seeming to be seriously considering her statement. Finally, he spoke.

"I can show you one piece now." He pressed an intercom button and spoke fluent Chinese. Then he stood and gestured toward the small table at the opposite end of his office placed directly in front of the one-way window. As he walked across the office, the door opened and the Chinese woman entered. She was carrying a carved teak box—transporting it, Jeffrey thought, as though she were the ring bearer at a wedding ceremony. She set the box down, opened it, and extracted a felt bag.

It first appeared to be three differently shaped blocks, all joined together by a chain. It was, unlike all the other jade they had seen, a yellowish-orange color. It seemed to Rachel to have an inner luminosity, as if history contributed to its radiance.

"Ch'ing Dynasty," Davidson said, staring at the objects. Both Jeffrey and Rachel noticed the intensity of his gaze. "Chops. The ancient Chinese symbol of signature, of individuality. These apparently belonged to a royal figure . . . and were originally discovered in a grave."

"In China?" Jeffrey asked.

"Obviously," Davidson said, hardly acknowledging the question.

"When?" Jeffrey persisted.

"When were they buried? Sometime during the period of the dynasty—1644 until early this century. Hard to be more specific."

"No, when were they found?"

"Oh, I should think probably a number of years ago. Their provenance is very much intact."

"I see." Jeffrey could barely hide his disappointment.

"Are there other pieces as well?" Rachel could push a bit too.

"Not today, I'm afraid. Perhaps in a day or so. I am in negotiations now for several objects."

"Then perhaps you will give us a telephone call. We're at the Kahala."

"Of course. It may be a while yet."

"We're prepared to be patient." She looked at him directly and tried to make her smile look genuine.

"Then perhaps you'd better tell me how to contact you on the mainland."

This she wasn't prepared for. She'd expended so much effort getting information about jade, she hadn't thought—nor had Jeffrey—how to protect her anonymity. So, she bit the bullet, reached into her purse, and handed Davidson her business card.

He examined it. "Your gallery . . . in Sherman Oaks. That's the San Fernando Valley. Am I correct?"

She wanted to slug him. Yes, it was the valley. Yes, a certain strange prejudice existed against the valley among those whose sphere of interest was limited to the West Side of Los Angeles. And yes, God damn it, that prejudice had made it all the way to Honolulu. He had—intentionally or not—hit her where she was vulnerable.

"Yes. Obviously you know Los Angeles."

"Oh, Miss Sabin." Davidson smiled gently. "I know a great many other things as well. Good afternoon to you both. Thank you for coming to my gallery."

As they got into the car, Jeffrey looked at his wristwatch. "Still two hours until the *Marara* sails. Let's drive down to Pearl Harbor and see what Eddie's turned up."

"Why do I think Eddie's found nothing?" Rachel asked as they began to weave their way through Honolulu's constant traffic.

"I think you're right. I'm also not sure Davidson's involved. At least not intentionally. Too much to lose."

"I don't know. There's something . . . something kind of obsessed about him. I kept feeling that under that glossy exterior there was a real zealot."

"All you art people are alike. A bunch of zealots."

"There are zealots and there are zealots," she said, almost to herself.

He was about to ask her to elaborate, but instead he concentrated on getting from the surface streets onto the Kamehameha Highway—Kam, as it was called locally. He crossed quickly to the fast lane and was about to congratulate himself on his adroit maneuvering when he looked up and saw the off-ramp sign for Pearl Harbor. He cursed and went to flip his turn indicator to move right—and instead hit the windshield wiper. He cursed again, found the turn indicator, and flipped it on. He moved right carefully.

He was still on Kam Highway, just yards short of the off ramp, when the van ahead of him slammed on its brakes. He slammed on his too, heard the screech of protest as the brakes took hold, and knew he was safe. He did not look into his rearview mirror, and so he did not see the pickup truck immediately behind him. It plowed into his rear, slamming him into the van directly in front of him. Jeffrey and Rachel both thumped the windshield, but their seat belts kept them from being hurt.

"Jesus. Just what I needed," Jeffrey muttered. He tried to open his door, but it was jammed shut. "You all right?"

"Fine." She tried her door and it too resisted, but finally opened. He crawled across, cursing the whole time.

Nobody was hurt, he could see that immediately. But the driver of the truck behind him was shouting, clearly blaming Jeffrey, and the two occupants of the van in front stood staring at him. They were all Chinese, all male, all angry.

Rachel was asking—practically begging—the volatile driver to calm down. Jeffrey joined in, and finally, in desperation, turned to the others to ask for help. Then it hit him. The man standing directly behind him, the man who had been a passenger in the pickup truck, was the same man who had followed Leilani and him on Sentosa Island and on the cable car in Singapore.

A police car, its red lights flashing, was headed in their direction. Jeffrey knew he was trapped, but couldn't figure out why. Then he decided what to do. He leaned over and whispered in Rachel's ear.

"Don't say a thing. Just slip back a little and then follow me when I run for it."

She looked up at him as if he was crazy.

"Quick, before the cops get here." He ran. She had no choice but to follow. In the confusion surrounding the arrival of the police cars—there were now two of them—they had a very short head start. About ten seconds' worth. They ran down the off ramp, cutting across the curve, heading toward Pearl Harbor.

Twice he glanced behind him to be sure Rachel was keeping up. The second time he saw the Chinese from Singapore come around the corner of the off ramp. And he saw the gun in his hand.

20

The road leading to the cargo area of Pearl Harbor is necessarily wide, yet it is also short. It is lined with a series of small buildings—military office complexes. Jeffrey, urging Rachel to run faster, darted down the path between the first two buildings and paused for breath.

"Why is that man chasing us?" Rachel asked between gasps for breath.

"I don't know. But he followed us in Singapore, and he's armed."

"I saw. What now?"

"Keep running. I saw a guard station just down the road a bit. If we can get there, we're safe." He was off, weaving his way down the path, cutting quickly behind another building. She followed, and they both kept glancing behind them.

They saw him once, as they turned right toward the entrance road and he appeared two buildings down, coming out of a side path. Jeffrey counted on his not using a gun while on a military base and kept going. In just over five minutes they ran up to the guard post and entered the compact building. There they came face to face with a tall man in a marine uniform, his identification prominently displayed on his sleeve.

"May I help you?" He was looking out the window, searching

for their car. Another starched marine appeared beside him.

"Has the *Marara* sailed yet?"

He traced his finger down the list on a clipboard. "Probably going right now."

"I need to talk to a customs agent at the ship. Martin . . . Leilani Martin."

"Mister, there must be two dozen customs agents at that ship. How do we find her?"

"I'll go look."

"That is against the rules. If you'll wait here, I'll call down to the pier office." He nodded in the direction of a small wood bench. Jeffrey and Rachel moved toward it, and Jeffrey felt an elbow in his ribs. He looked up and there, less than fifty yards down the road, he saw their pursuer, standing beside one of the buildings, staring at the guard shack, obviously unsure what to do next.

"We're safe," Jeffrey whispered.

"For now," she added, sitting down, still winded.

Half an hour later, Jeffrey looked up and saw Eddie and Leilani being driven by a navy man toward the guardhouse. They were riding in what to Jeffrey looked like a golf cart. It would have fit nicely into any resort but for its stark navy gray. Leilani seemed annoyed to see them there, but Eddie greeted them warmly. He looked around and asked the obvious: "Where's your car?"

"Folded between a pickup truck and a van on Kam Highway. We ran here."

"We were chased here," Rachel interrupted. Leilani looked at them evenly, as if unsure how to react. Eddie simply waited for an explanation. Quickly, Jeffrey told them what had happened.

"Where is he now?" Leilani asked, looking out onto the roadway.

"Gone, obviously." Rachel's frustration was getting the better of her.

"That does it," Eddie said, turning to Leilani. "The stuff was on the ship."

"Was?" Jeffrey looked puzzled.

"We've gone over it and over it. If it's there we couldn't find it. They've practically ripped the goddamn thing apart."

Leilani cleared them with the guards and they all crowded onto the golf cart. It took only a few minutes before they turned around the corner of a long warehouse and were on the dockside by the ship. From their vantage point, the freighter looked enormous, a black, ominous, floating city which, because of its width, was visible only as a huge bulk. They could not see up its sides, and only a small portion of the superstructure was visible.

There must have been twenty customs agents in uniform standing near the steps leading up the side of the great ship. They stood in small clusters. At their center, holding a clipboard, was Carl Spelling. As Jeffrey and Rachel approached, Spelling looked up, surprised to see them again.

They were introduced to the man standing next to Spelling: a florid man named Mark O'Brien, head of the Honolulu U.S. Customs office. Sweat streaked his cheeks, and he wiped it with a handkerchief. He did not appear at all happy.

He had reason. The search had yielded absolutely nothing except a small amount of marijuana and cocaine, which, given the size of the ship, was less than would normally be hidden on board by crew members. The expenditure of man-hours and effort was considerable, and the waste would not go unnoticed by his economy-conscious bosses.

"So, this is the man who figured out it was the *Marara*," O'Brien said pointedly as he shook hands with Jeffrey. "Nice try. Even Leilani here agreed it was the place we'd find the jade. Not so, it turns out."

The battalion of customs inspectors dispersed, leaving only Leilani and Spelling. Jeffrey, Rachel, and Eddie stood by, watching them go and observing the *Marara* in the final stages of setting sail for San Francisco. Finally, there was a great blast from the ship and the winches began pulling the boarding stairs up.

"Shit," Eddie remarked. "I thought we had something. I

can't understand it. I saw these guys take it apart. The captain was furious."

"Maybe the jade is already ashore," Jeffrey offered.

"How? No one got off the ship. The crew was confined, the ship was searched. Nobody jumped overboard."

Leilani and Spelling joined them, accompanied this time by a short, friendly Chinese man they introduced as Roger Chow.

"The third member of our team," Spelling explained.

"Some team," Chow added. "We didn't even get a base hit."

"Roger's a baseball fanatic," Leilani told them.

"A shutout, then." Jeffrey smiled.

"Don't you think you'd better go and check what happened to your car?" Leilani was rummaging in her purse, looking intently into it as she spoke. Finally, she extracted a stick of gum.

"I'll go with them," Eddie offered.

"Somebody's going to have to give Budget Rent-a-Car one hell of an explanation," Rachel said. "Somebody besides us. I hope." There were no offers of assistance.

"Did you get the collision coverage?" Spelling inquired.

"Yes," Jeffrey said, "but can you imagine the forms I'm going to have to fill out? All that and provide an excuse for abandoning the car?"

"They're used to it," Leilani said, delicately unwrapping her gum. Jeffrey was struck by the change in her since Singapore, and decided it was because she was now on her home turf, and more often than not accustomed to being in charge.

The ship was moving, nudged out of its nest by two straining Navy tugs. It began sliding slowly into the center of Pearl Harbor. They all watched. Finally, its great bulk was clear of the long dock. Light was fading fast, and as Jeffrey looked out across the bay, he saw one of the last tourist boats leave the *Arizona* Memorial. He could see the white slabs of marble and most of the twenty-one windows; he noticed Rachel was staring at it too. Then the flag began its descent, and one by one the lights on the memorial itself came on.

"Let's get out of here," Spelling muttered loud enough for

them all to hear. He turned and started toward the small parking lot across the road from the warehouse. The others followed. As they were about to turn the corner near the building, Jeffrey stopped and looked back at the memorial.

Then it hit him. "It's there . . . ," he said. "On the *Arizona* Memorial. I mean—under it."

"What the hell are you talking about?" Leilani seemed uncharacteristically abrupt, probably still irritated by the dead end the *Marara* turned out to be.

"It's on the memorial. Probably in a package right down at the bottom," Jeffrey said.

They all stared at him as if he was mad.

"Eddie . . . Leilani . . . are you sure Davidson is involved in all of this?"

"Possibly, but we haven't got the evidence," Leilani answered.

"I'm sure he is," Eddie said. "His shipping business is in a mess, he's desperate for money. But she's right, we haven't got the evidence."

"The evidence is right over there," Jeffrey said, pointing at the memorial. "I'm sure of it."

"How did you arrive at this brilliant conclusion?" Leilani asked, her voice coldly skeptical.

"Simple. The answer was in Davidson's office. I just didn't know it."

"Today, when we were looking at jade?" Rachel asked.

"No. During the art show last night."

"What were you doing in his office?" Now even Eddie was beginning to sound puzzled.

"I thought it was the public bathroom. When I opened the door I could see I was mistaken . . . but I could also see a small bathroom near his desk. The door was open, the light was on. So I went for a pee."

"And?" Roger Chow, alone among the others, seemed genuinely interested. Eddie was curious but noncommittal. Leilani and Spelling looked dubious, to say the least.

"Wait a minute. You were in his office today?" Now Spelling was getting agitated.

"Just shopping," Rachel shot back at him.

"When I was going to the bathroom," Jeffrey continued as if he hadn't been interrupted, "I automatically turned off the light and walked into the dark office. I accidentally kicked his wastebasket and knocked it over." He paused, trying to be as precise as possible. "I found a little souvenir. A piece of the *Arizona* Memorial. It had been thrown away. Now what would a man like Davidson be doing with something like that if he wasn't using it for something?"

"Jesus," Eddie muttered. Leilani, Spelling, and Chow said nothing.

"Somebody probably left it in the gallery or something. I mean nobody in their right mind would put jade in a place like that." Spelling was adamant.

"Why not?" Rachel disagreed. "And who said he's in his right mind anyway?"

"It's worth checking out." Eddie, as if to hide his embarrassment, looked down and shuffled his feet.

"Oh what the hell. But it's not worth calling O'Brien or bringing in anyone else. We've screwed this up enough already." But Leilani's instincts pushed her toward the memorial, Jeffrey was certain of that.

"I'm not guessing," Jeffrey insisted. They all looked at him. "Not really."

21

Leilani's Treasury Department ID had given them immediate access to Ford Island, with nothing more than a shrug of disinterest by the marine guard at the boarding ramp for the ferry. At the landing, they turned right, in the direction of the memorial.

Jeffrey was in the seat beside Leilani. Rachel and Eddie sat silently in the cramped backseat of the old but well-maintained Volkswagen. Carl Spelling had excused himself to get started on the paperwork from the abortive *Marara* expedition. Leilani had promised to call him at the airport customs office within the hour, and Spelling promised to try and join them later. Roger Chow was right behind them in his own car.

Leilani drove directly toward the memorial, which was located offshore, immediately behind two homes, both secluded from the waterfront by trees. The houses were brightly lit, and in one yard they could see a barbecue, already lit, and a man and two children standing near it.

"Keep going," Eddie said. Leilani nodded as they turned and headed back toward the ferry. A short distance later they came upon a long, low building with a blue and gold sign on its roof: THE ARIZONA CLUB. They could hear the steady twang of country-and-western music, the sounds of broken hearts and lonesome trails.

"Here. This will do," Leilani said. She pulled into an empty parking space next to the club, right by three pay telephones anchored on the side of the building and lit by a dim overhead bulb. Roger pulled in beside them. They walked the rest of the way, staying on the roadway until they could see the lights of the memorial. Then they moved off the pavement and onto the rocky sand close to the water's edge.

Most of the waterfront was open, but there was one secluded place directly between the houses and the memorial that was overgrown with shrubs, some of them six feet tall.

Eddie slid down the slight incline to the water. Jeffrey followed. Leilani and Rachel waited.

"Now what?" Jeffrey asked. The notion of swimming to a vessel containing over a thousand bodies was not one either man wanted to contemplate.

"There's a little kid's sailboat—a dinghy—beside the garage of the first house." Eddie pointed. "Nobody will see us take it. We can use that to get out to the *Arizona*."

They crawled back up the incline and explained their idea to Leilani and Rachel. Leilani objected immediately.

"Look. Roger and I can't be caught stealing things like that," she protested.

"You're not going to do it. Anyhow, we'll return it and nobody will know," Jeffrey said, walking away. Eddie followed.

They were back with the dinghy within minutes.

"Where's Leilani?" Jeffrey asked as they slid the boat down the incline.

"Gone to call Spelling," Rachel replied. "Now what?"

"Now we get the boat into the water," Jeffrey said, "and paddle out to the memorial. Only there are no paddles. We'll have to use our hands. You armed?" he asked Eddie.

"Yeah. I'm not supposed to be but I am."

"I am too," Roger volunteered.

"So's Leilani," Jeffrey added.

"How'd you know that?" Rachel asked.

"I had her purse on my lap . . . if you can call that thing she's always carrying a purse. I could feel the gun weighing it down," he said. "So we're well protected . . ."

By the time Leilani returned, they had it figured out. Rachel would wait onshore, with plenty of change for the telephone, and Roger's car keys. Roger volunteered to stay with her.

Jeffrey, Eddie, and Leilani set out in the little dinghy. It was less than thirty yards to the submerged ship, and only a few yards further to the monument. Without oars, their progress was slow, but between the gentle tide and their arms, they were soon passing over the huge ship. Jeffrey guided the boat to a point just forward of the Memorial Chapel. He was within arm's length of the memorial itself, and could see the metal stairs built along the side, when the little boat scraped the sunken ship's deck and stopped.

The spotlights along the sides of the memorial flooded the sky, illuminating the dinghy and its passengers. Jeffrey looked down. The metal deck of the *Arizona* was less than two feet below the surface.

"I can get out and walk from here. Then I'll pull the dinghy behind me. Without my weight it'll move easily."

"Hurry," Eddie muttered. "Somebody's bound to see us."

Jeffrey rolled up his pants, then started to remove his sneakers.

"Better leave them on," Leilani advised. "You can get cut up on this rusted metal." Jeffrey stepped onto the USS *Arizona* and felt for his footing, half expecting to fall through the aging metal. He wondered how long it had been since the last time a person had actually walked on that deck.

The dinghy bobbed free and he pulled it behind him. Eddie and Leilani scrambled quickly up the few rungs onto the memorial and Jeffrey, still standing on the *Arizona*, raised the dinghy up to them.

The angle of the spotlights, shining straight up and out, provided a dim illumination that made moving about the inside of the memorial easy. Jeffrey quickly walked to the door of the small office. It was locked. He looked around and could just make out an electrical panel beside the door. He opened it. There were two switches, one marked INTERIOR LIGHTS, the other SOUND EFFECTS.

"When's Spelling coming?" he asked Leilani.

"In less than an hour, as soon as he turns in all the paperwork on the *Marara* search. It won't be long." She stepped toward the open mooring area where the tourist boats tied up.

Jeffrey walked to the mooring. Directly across the bay was the berth the *Marara* had vacated a few hours earlier. "If the jade's here and they come to get it, this should be the spot. It's the only possible place on the ship."

"It'd have to be if they took it off the *Marara*. Nobody could swim to the other side, not during daylight," Eddie whispered.

"Underwater?" Jeffrey asked.

"Even underwater," Eddie insisted. "They'd never make it around the whole ship. Too much to do, too little time."

They could hear only the slap of water against the pilings of the memorial, and the occasional splash of a small fish breaking the surface. They waited. Finally, Jeffrey looked down at his watch. It was eleven forty-five p.m.

"It won't be long now."

"How do you know that?" Leilani seemed genuinely surprised.

"All over Ford's Island—and Pearl Harbor for that matter—the guard changes at midnight. And the little souvenir in Alfred Davidson's office had the number 'twenty-four hundred' written on it."

"Military time," Eddie added.

"I know. Why didn't you say that before?" Leilani asked. Both men could sense her anger.

"I thought I had," Jeffrey lied.

"I sure as hell don't remember it." Leilani walked slowly back to the chapel.

"I don't think you did mention it," Eddie whispered.

"I know I didn't. There's a rotten apple—Spelling. When you went to the gallery with him, did Davidson pretend not to know·him?"

"Yeah. Kept forgetting his name. Mine too."

"I saw them through the one-way mirror in Davidson's office. Davidson shot him a couple glances, and then when he and Davidson walked away from you, they walked in separate directions."

"So?"

"I saw Davidson give him the high sign from across the room, motioning toward you, Leilani, and Rachel. Spelling immediately returned to you. I think he was supposed to be listening. That's what Davidson was telling him to do."

"Could be," Eddie whispered. "And you didn't want to tell her," he added, nodding in Leilani's direction.

"I don't think she'd believe it, and Spelling could possibly get away with it. Technically he hasn't done anything . . . unless there are things we don't know about. And maybe I'm completely wrong."

Crawling on their stomachs, Eddie and Jeffrey moved toward the mooring area, taking care to stay in the darker shadows. Leilani stood behind them, watching. Jeffrey turned and looked up at her. "Be careful," she said to them. "I'll be backing you up."

They didn't have to wait long. Almost on the stroke of midnight Jeffrey spotted an underwater flashlight beam. Eddie saw it a second later. "Somebody's here," he said quietly, but loud enough so that Leilani could hear. He looked back and she nodded. They waited.

Finally there was a loud metallic thud, and suddenly a series of bubbles surfaced just below the mooring. A large package bubbled to the surface, protected by a flotation collar. Then a diver surfaced and swam toward the mooring itself. Jeffrey and Eddie—with Leilani immediately to their rear—watched as the hand reached up and threw a rope over the mooring post, then disappeared.

"Jesus. You were right," Eddie whispered. "Stay behind me. I'm going to pull up the package." Eddie crawled out to the edge of the mooring and began hauling in the rope.

Jeffrey crawled after him. They were poised to pull the package onto the deck when everything went wrong. The gunshot was behind them, not in front of them where they'd expected it. They heard Leilani swear and drop to the deck. Jeffrey could see her crawling away from them, toward the chapel. The next shot hit the mooring post just above Eddie's head.

22

Jeffrey and Eddie scrambled for cover, Eddie dragging the package along with him. Another package bubbled to the surface, followed by a diver's arm and head. After the package was placed on the landing area, the head and arm disappeared underwater. An underwater light went on seconds later.

"Leilani . . . you all right?" Jeffrey shouted.

"Fine. I can see you."

"Where did the shot come from?"

"Somewhere behind me. We've got company."

Jeffrey crouched and ran for the small office enclosure, knocking over a chair and a flag stand. He stood up and quickly flipped both switches in the electrical panel.

The *Arizona* Memorial erupted into noisy life. The lights in the interior suddenly came on, and the whistle of descending bombs, the blast of explosions, the buzz of diving Japanese Zeros, and the wail of sirens suddenly shattered the night air, sending the sound of history screaming across the water.

"The diver," Eddie shouted at him. "Cover us, Leilani!" He ran to the edge of the small dock, spotted the diver in the water less than five feet away, and jumped. Jeffrey could see the diver's black-hooded head dive beneath the surface, and saw the knife in his hand. Eddie landed on the diver, pulling off his mask and mouthpiece in one jarring move. The head pulled back and the thrashing began. It was too dark to see who it was, but Jeffrey thought he knew.

He was about to jump into the water too, when another shot rang out, slamming into the marble wall immediately to his right. He crashed to the floor, hitting his leg on the arm of an overturned wooden chair. He cursed, then realized that, unless he was ready to jump into the water—and risk letting whoever was shooting at them get away—he was trapped.

"Leilani!" he shouted.

"Someone's here with us," she yelled back at him. "I'm trying to see who, but the light's too bright."

Jeffrey raced to the wall panel, then looked to make sure he had the right switch before turning off the interior lights. As he crouched down again he could see the flashing red and white lights of a shore patrol boat heading in their direction from the distant opening of the harbor.

To his right was the water, where Eddie and the diver were fighting. To his immediate left, Leilani was hiding in the small chapel. He looked again and could now see Eddie with a hammerlock around the diver's head, towing his limp body to the mooring. Jeffrey stood up and ran for the chapel, knowing that he would soon have Eddie as a backup, and that Leilani was trapped in the small room by whoever was now in the memorial with them.

The scream of diving aircraft and a deafening explosion accompanied him across the length of the memorial. He slipped and skidded the last several feet on his back, painfully wrenching his shoulder.

"God damn you," Leilani said to him.

"I figured you needed help," he muttered.

"You figured wrong," she said evenly.

"Well, somebody's shooting at you," he said, peering into the darkness.

"You don't get it, do you." It was not a question.

Then, suddenly, he did. Leilani's gun was held securely in

both her hands. It was aimed directly at him. What puzzled him now was the expression on her face. It wasn't one of triumph or anger. Pain was more like it.

"Once you got into this, I . . . I . . . tried, I really did. Everything to keep you out of it. After Singapore, I thought you were gone forever. That was no accident on Kam Highway. Now it's too late."

"That was you shooting at us."

"Not *at* you," she nodded her head. "Just near you."

Jeffrey sat on the floor, his legs stretched out before him, looking directly at her, shaking his head.

Finally, he spoke. "Why?"

"Carl figured it out first. Then we met Davidson."

"And the offer was too good to refuse?"

"Yes."

"Not anymore, Leilani."

She ignored him. "Turn over. Lie on your stomach. Put your arms behind your back."

He did as he was told. She took a small coil of rope from the base of the flagpole and tied his arms.

"You haven't got the guts," he said to her, barely containing his anger and frustration.

"To kill you? You're right. That isn't my job . . . it's somebody else's. This whole thing is a disaster."

"Was fucking me part of your job too?"

She paused, but only briefly: "Not really."

Jeffrey could see Eddie hauling the diver onto the dock with one arm, and pulling the package behind him with the other. Eddie leaned down and pulled off the diver's hood. It was Spelling. He was barely conscious, and there was blood coming from a tear on the arm of his wetsuit. He looked up dazed—then, as Leilani came into focus, he smiled weakly.

"Check him for weapons while I pull the package out of the water," Eddie said, turning his back to Leilani.

"All right," she said evenly. Eddie went for the package without looking back. Leilani followed him. Jeffrey yelled.

"Look out, Eddie! It's her!"

It was too late. Eddie had picked up the package and come face-to-muzzle with her. He walked slowly back onto the deck of the memorial, soaking wet and looking ashamed of himself.

"Carl! Get up! You've got to help. The shore patrol is coming right at us. We've got to get out of here." Now she was in charge, and there was no doubting her authority.

Somehow, Spelling stood up. With his one good arm he lifted the dinghy out of the memorial and into the water. He swung down the ladder and roughly took Jeffrey by the arm.

Leilani, covering Eddie, ordered him toward the ladder. As she did so, she hissed at Spelling, "I thought you weren't coming. We agreed to call it off tonight."

"He ordered me," Spelling muttered. "I didn't have any alternative."

"Like hell you didn't. Hurry!" Leilani whispered angrily.

Jeffrey stumbled down the rungs and landed with a splash face first in the shallow water on the deck of the ship, cutting his forehead on a piece of metal. He struggled to his feet and stepped into the dinghy. Eddie was next, and Leilani came last, still holding the two packages. The boat stuck again. Leilani cursed, crawled out, and shoved it free. They swung into the darkness between the memorial and Ford's Island just as the shore patrol's high-intensity spotlight began sweeping the area. The memorial hid them, sheltering them in darkness.

"I'm jumping in," Spelling said. "The water's shallow and I can walk. I'll pull the boat." In a couple of minutes, they were onshore.

They were met by the Chinese man Jeffrey had last seen on Kam Highway.

"You're not supposed to come ashore here with the jade," he scowled.

"We didn't have any choice," Leilani said. "Where are they?"

"Where's Rachel?" Jeffrey looked as if he were about to explode.

"I'm saving her. In case we need her. Where are the packages?"

"Where's Roger?" Spelling asked.

"Busy." He seemed about to say more, but Jeffrey interrupted him.

"Where is Rachel?"

"Tied up behind those bushes. With her mouth taped shut. Now shut yours." He turned to Spelling. "Where are the goddamned packages?"

"Right here." He tried to lift one but winced in pain. "I cut my arm on the *Arizona*."

"Foolish of you," the Chinese man muttered. "You . . . Leilani . . . get the packages. My car is just over there, on the road. Take them there."

Leilani glared at him, the hatred and the fear showing in her otherwise expressionless dark eyes. Then she picked up both packages and started up the hill, slowed by their weight. The others followed.

They found Rachel bound and gagged, sitting on a mound of sand in the tall shrubs. Spelling yanked off her gag, then withdrew his knife, reached down, and cut the ropes binding her ankles. She struggled to rise, but could not. With his good arm Spelling jerked her upright and motioned her ahead. She looked at Jeffrey, and at the blood running down his forehead.

"You all right?"

"Fine. Just a cut."

"Move. Don't talk," the Chinese man said, shoving the muzzle of his pistol in Jeffrey's back.

It was the van Jeffrey had hit on the Kam Highway hours before. Its rear was severely dented, the bumper folded in the middle. But the door was on the side panel, and Spelling, with his one good arm, slid it open.

Leilani saw him first. Her look of horror was unmistakable. "God damn it, Lui, you promised there'd be no killing."

"He had to go," the Chinese said coolly. "So do these others. Only not here."

Jeffrey, Rachel, and Eddie now saw too. The body of Roger Chow, bound, gagged, and shot through the head, lay on the floor of the van. Roger's glasses had slipped sideways, giving him an almost comical appearance in death.

"He told you no killing," Leilani insisted.

"That's what he said when you were there. He told me otherwise."

Leilani said nothing. Spelling, peering at the body, seemed unconcerned. He had Eddie's gun, and held it trained on the small cluster of people standing outside the van.

"Okay, one by one you get in the van. You," Lui said, pointing his gun at Leilani, "tie their hands. I'll put the tape on their mouths so they don't start shouting. Spelling, you guard. One wrong move from any of you and you'll get it here."

"Here or wherever doesn't matter much, does it?" Jeffrey muttered. He turned, paused for a second, and then crashed into Spelling, slamming into his cut arm. Spelling's trigger finger was too tight—his gun fired into the night air.

Eddie dived for the back of the van, stumbled, and fought to regain his balance. Jeffrey and Rachel watched in terror as the man named Lui aimed at Eddie's back.

Before he could fire, there was another shot and Lui, a look of absolute and terminal surprise on his face, went down. Jeffrey and Rachel turned to see what had happened. Leilani had shot him.

"Jesus Christ, what are you doing?" Spelling shouted.

"Shut up or I'll shoot you, too," she yelled back at him.

Spelling went down under the combined weight of Jeffrey and Rachel. Jeffrey grabbed his gun, and handed it to Eddie as he reappeared from behind the van.

"What in hell?" Eddie was thoroughly confused.

"Don't move," Leilani said to him. "You two either," she said to Jeffrey and Rachel. "Carl, get up and stand by the packages."

"What in hell are you doing?" Spelling could barely get up off the ground. Neither Jeffrey nor Rachel nor Eddie offered to help him. Finally, Leilani gave him her hand and pulled him up.

"It's over, Carl. Davidson promised good money . . . no danger, no killing. Then he brought in Lui. The killing is over . . . so is this whole thing."

"Over?" Spelling didn't seem to understand.

"Over," Leilani said. As if to convince herself, she said it again: "Over. Finished. We'll never get off this island now. The shore patrol will be here in seconds. There are already people on the memorial."

"What about us?" Eddie asked.

"It's our word against yours," Leilani said evenly. "Nobody will believe you. Carl and I followed you here . . . and saved you from Lui. Lui works for Davidson."

"Does he?" Jeffrey asked.

"You bet," Leilani said. "And I can prove it. We don't. Not anymore." Then, with a half-smile of regret, she stared at Jeffrey. "It was going fine until you came along."

"Singapore," Jeffrey suddenly remembered. "The night I met you."

"We had competition for the jade," she said. "They came after me. Thanks to you, they didn't get me. Now I'm returning the favor."

"But . . . Lui. Him." Jeffrey nodded in the direction of the Chinese man's body. "You spotted him in Singapore. Didn't you know who he was?"

"Not then," she said. "I didn't find out until I got back here. Now help me get the packages into the van."

They heard the siren and saw the reflection of the lights before they saw the shore patrol jeep. No one moved. The packages remained on the pavement, their flotation collars still in place, but now deflated.

"What do we do now?" Rachel asked.

"We all stay right here. When they show up I'll show my ID and the packages. Then I'm going to turn the jade in and end this thing once and for all."

"And lose all that money?" Spelling was incredulous.

"Right. And save our asses."

The jeep pulled up in front of the van. Two armed shore patrol men and a woman jumped out, their weapons drawn.

"Take it easy!" Leilani yelled at them. "I'm a U.S. Customs officer. We've got it under control."

"Not quite," Jeffrey muttered to himself.

23

He had known rooms like this existed, but Jeffrey had never seen one until now. It was perfect, a rare matchup between fantasy and reality. The president's government-issue photograph in a government-issue frame was on the wall directly behind the head of the table. There was an American flag, with a polished gold eagle atop its stand, bearing silent witness to what was transpiring in this conference room on the top floor of the Federal Building in downtown Honolulu.

The paneled walls formed a monotone interrupted by windows with a spectacular view of the Pacific Ocean. It was all an attempt to convey elegance and power, and it was a failure because all the work had been contracted out to the lowest bidder.

The conference table was long and highly polished. An assortment of people—some familiar, some not—were seated there. The meeting was chaired by a businesslike man named Petersen, who was with the State Department. They all knew what Petersen was doing in Honolulu—he was there, as Eddie succinctly put it, as a "Marcos watcher," charged with monitoring the behavior of Hawaii's most famous exiles in residence. Eddie, Jeffrey, and Rachel all suspected that he wasn't really from State. He was, as Eddie cynically stated, "one of Charlie's Indians trying to get the goods on the Marcoses."

They had all—Jeffrey, Rachel, Eddie, Leilani, and Spelling— met separately with Petersen, and now they had all been assembled to bear witness to what was about to be declared.

The last two days had been chaotic, with consultations back and forth between Honolulu and Washington, Washington and Singapore, and on and on. Jeffrey had not been at all surprised to find C. D. Lee, pin-striped and proper, seated at the table as a representative of the government of Singapore.

Jeffrey was seated between Rachel and Eddie. Opposite them were Leilani, Spelling, and their perspiring boss, Mark O'Brien. Farther down the table sat Alfred Davidson, flanked by his lawyers.

Petersen looked around the room, mentally counting heads and consulting his notes. "We're short just one person," he said, and, as if on cue, the missing man arrived.

Jeffrey was astonished. It was William Wong How. He was even more astonished when Petersen introduced the final attendee as "Mr. Chaing Lu of the People's Republic of China."

"Son of a bitch," Jeffrey whispered to himself. Lu took his place, choosing the chair beside C. D. Lee. Petersen sat down at the head of the table, immediately to the right of the naval commander in charge of base security at Pearl Harbor. He cleared his throat, consulted his notes once again, and finally began speaking.

"The smuggled jade is being returned to the Singapore government today. Mr. C. D. Lee has been authorized to take possession of it and will be returning it in turn to Mr. Chaing Lu of the People's Republic of China."

Lee nodded, and unsuccessfully tried not to appear too self-important. Lu merely nodded, then looked directly at Jeffrey.

"The matter ends there," Petersen said. "You have all been interviewed these last two days, by myself and by attorneys and law-enforcement personnel of the federal government. Accusations have been made, some of which we believe"—he looked down at his notes, smoothed his tie, and continued—"some of which we officially believe will be of severe damage to the United States' dealings with other countries if it should become a public matter."

Jeffrey fidgeted in his chair, and exchanged glances with Eddie.

"No charges have been brought against any of you involved in this affair, and no charges will be brought."

Jeffrey had expected it. So had Eddie and Rachel. If Leilani and Spelling were feeling any relief, they did not show it. Davidson sat impassively, his face devoid of expression.

So Davidson would remain as he was—insulated and obsessed, with his actions carefully concealed, but no longer quite well enough. Everybody present knew that he had been behind the smuggling, that he had employed Lui, Leilani, and Spelling, and that this hadn't been his only operation. It was his largest, but there were others: the dead pet-shop owner was proof of that.

Where absolute proof was required, it had vanished: How had the jade gotten from the *Marara* to its hiding place across the bay beneath the *Arizona*? Eddie knew. So did Jeffrey, Rachel, C. D. Lee, and the unhappy State Department spokesman Petersen. Davidson, Leilani, and Spelling knew too, but they weren't talking.

There was no evidence, but what those who wanted to prove it and those who were determined to keep it secret all knew was that there had been one extra able-bodied seaman on the *Marara* when it left Singapore. His presence had been known to the captain, a long-time employee of TransPac, but hidden from the crew. There was even a notation of a ship-to-shore radio conversation between someone on the *Marara* and someone in Davidson's office only hours before the ship was due in Pearl Harbor. One of the customs agents had noted its presence in the captain's log. Still, it proved nothing.

The extra seaman had been there as a safeguard. As it became evident that U.S. Customs would be thoroughly searching the ship, he became necessary. He took the two packages, trailed them off the side of the *Marara* just before it docked, and went overboard with them. He did as he was told: Swam across to the *Arizona*, deposited the packages, and then quickly disappeared. But Davidson had been unwilling—despite the risk of attempting to recover it too soon—to let his treasure stay underwater a moment longer than necessary. He was not, everyone knew, a patient or a trusting man.

"That does not mean that officials of this government, and the agencies involved, do not have their suspicions or concerns about future activities," Petersen said, shuffling his papers. "To this end, certain government employees involved in this affair will be reassigned to new positions in their respective agencies. The others . . . Miss Sabin, Mr. Dean, Mr. Alvaraz . . . are free to leave, and have been advised that their discretion in this matter is crucial."

Petersen paused and looked directly at each of them. When he came to Alfred Davidson he resumed his speech. "Mr. Davidson has received an unofficial apology for any inconvenience caused to him by this affair, and has agreed to drop the matter. You are all free to go."

"What bullshit," Jeffrey whispered to Eddie, who nodded in agreement.

They were aware that Rachel was staring—no, glaring—at Petersen, barely hiding her disgust. She turned to them, speaking just above a whisper. "That's what prominent citizens get—an 'apology.' Lesser mortals like us aren't entitled to such gestures."

With an audible sigh, Petersen stood up, slammed his leather-bound notebook shut, and walked out of the room, followed by the naval commander.

Davidson and his attorneys followed. Leilani, Spelling, and O'Brien stood briefly, and began talking among themselves. C. D. Lee and Lu were in a huddle of their own by a window.

"Let's get the hell out of here," Jeffrey said. Rachel and Eddie followed him out of the room to the elevator bank. As he started out the door, Jeffrey turned and looked toward Leilani. When their glances met, she quickly turned her back to him. He shook his head.

"What I can't understand is who is doing what to whom on the government level," Rachel said as they walked to the parking lot.

"What I've been told—unofficially, of course—is that some of the jade was part of China's national treasure. It was being smuggled out of the country, through Singapore, to the States. China has its own criminals, but the government is loath to admit there are problems in the people's paradise. Big money was involved, and Davidson, of course, was skimming off the best pieces. The Singapore people are scared, because they stand to gain so much when the Chinese take over Hong Kong. The U.S. and China are trying to smooth things over. That's it."

"And because of the delicate diplomatic relations between the countries involved," Jeffrey continued for him, "it is in all of their best interests not to make a public affair of it."

"In other words," Rachel added, "shut the whole thing up."

"Tight," Eddie said.

"I can accept that, but I can't accept Leilani, Spelling, and Davidson getting off so easily."

"Leilani and Spelling are finished as far as government work is concerned. No conviction, of course, but such strong suspicions nevertheless wreck careers."

"And Davidson is off the hook."

"Off," Eddie agreed, "but I suspect still vulnerable. Roger Chow is dead. Lui too. Leilani and Spelling can tell a lot about him. That, I think, will keep him really worried."

"I've met Mr. Lu of the People's Republic," Jeffrey told them. "Several times in fact."

"Lu was also the threatening Mr. How, that right?" Eddie, as usual, had figured it out right away.

Jeffrey nodded. "I actually think he was using me to try to get to Leilani—or at least to what she knew."

Rachel smiled. She too had guessed Chaing Lu's other identity, by watching Jeffrey's reaction to him in the conference room.

They watched as Davidson drove out of the parking lot in his Mercedes convertible, followed less than a minute later by Leilani and Spelling in her VW bug.

"And your car?" Eddie asked Jeffrey.

"Last I saw, it was on Kam Highway. Petersen and his people are taking care of it. Rachel did the honors this time," he laughed, motioning toward a Camaro convertible parked in the shade.

"We haven't heard the last," Eddie said. "I'll bet you."

"I agree," Jeffrey added.

"I hope so." Rachel was in the car, ready to go back to the Kahala and the final two days of their vacation.

Two months later, Rachel and Jeffrey were sitting in their living room, relishing the last of a late spring rain, which was turning Los Angeles from smoggy brown to bright blue and green. Jeffrey was reading the *Times,* and Rachel was deep into *ArtForum.* He was reading a detailed prediction of the next day's weather when he saw, out of the corner of his eye, the small story on the adjoining page.

"Oh my God," he said. "One of the shoes has dropped."

Rachel looked up.

"Carl Spelling was indicted for smuggling. Jade again."

"And?"

"And died. Drowned. An accident, it says here."

"I doubt it," she said. "I really do."

The other shoe dropped several weeks later. Eddie Alvaraz turned up for dinner one night with a clipping from the society pages of the *Honolulu Bulletin.* Jeffrey could only laugh, mostly from the embarrassment and guilt a certain memory evoked in him. Rachel shook her head in dismay.

"Leilani moves fast—real fast," Eddie told them.

Alfred Davidson had married Leilani Martin in a private